BEAUTY AND THE LUMBERJACKS

A CONTEMPORARY REVERSE HAREM ROMANCE

LEE SAVINO

This book is dedicated to second trimester hormones and Maggie Ryan, who edited my first crazy reverse harem I wrote the last time I was pregnant.

FREE BOOK

Get a secret Berserker book, Bred by the Berserkers (only to
the awesomesauce fans on Lee's email list)
Click here to get started...

BEAUTY AND THE LUMBERJACKS

After this logging season, I'm never having sex again. Because: reasons.

But first, I have a gig earning room and board and ten thousand dollars by 'entertaining' 8 lumberjacks. Eight strong and strapping Paul Bunyan types, big enough to break me in two.

There's Lincoln, the leader, the stern, silent type...

Jagger, the Kurt Cobain look-alike, with a soul full of music and rockstar moves...

Elon & Oren, ginger twins who share everything...

Saint, the quiet genius with a monster in his pants...

Roy and Tommy, who just want to watch...

And Mason, who hates me and won't say why, but on his night tries to break me with pleasure

They own me: body, mind and orgasms.

But when they discover my secret--the reason I'm hiding from the world—everything changes.

1

S ierra

A FROSTBITTEN BREEZE slices through my hoodie, pinches my skin and sweeps on, sending trash flying down the sidewalk. I hunch my head and clutch my backpack to my chest to give me a buffer against the wind. Even summer is chilly this far north.

Vacant buildings turn a blind eye to my progress. Halfway across an empty parking lot, a wave of sickness hits. I hurry to an alley and dry-heave. There's nothing in my stomach but it cramps anyway, muscles tightening like a fist around emptiness. I slump against the dirty wall.

Not now. I don't need to be sick on top of everything. I fumble in my stained backpack for my water bottle and swish some tepid liquid in my mouth. I don't know if the metallic taste is from the tap water, old plastic, or some mysterious illness I've caught on top of everything else. It's probably just hunger. It's been way, way too long since I had a good meal.

The roar of motorcycle pipes sends me deep into the alley. *They've found me.* I plaster myself against the wall, garbage at my feet, and hold my breath. My eyes close like a child. *If I can't see the monster, it can't find me.*

The pipes fade into a truck's hiss and rumble. *They're not here.* I've run north, too far into the middle of nowhere. The Hell Riders will search the towns of their territory, moving south. No one in their right mind would run north.

My hands shake, half from weakness, half from fear.

After a few minutes leaning against the wall, I make myself get moving. Across the street and up ahead, a big sign announces, 'Randy's Place.' I cross the street, an obstacle course of broken pavement and half-frozen puddles, wincing as the mud stains my tennis shoes. I'm not at my best to go begging for a job. But I won't need these shoes to be a stripper.

As I hit the sidewalk, a truck rolls by, close enough to spatter my jeans with dirty water. Just the final sprint in a run of shitty bad luck. I plan to strip down to my bra and underwear before the interview. Randy wasn't too happy to see me yesterday; I'm not sure why I think today will be different. Desperation and delusion caused by an empty stomach.

If he would just give me a chance, I know I have a pretty enough face. With more food, I'll have all the lady goods I need to barter with. But I need cash to buy food, and to get cash, I need a night on the pole.

If I were smart, I'd move on from this tiny town, where the best employment option is a rundown dance bar catering to truckers. But I don't have the money to run far and can't risk poking my head up in a nearby town. The Hell Riders own this part of the country.

My only hope of hiding is this pit of mud and broken pavement, too small to support much more than a couple of gas stations, a general store that sells everything from chainsaws to underwear, a dingy 24-hour diner, and Randy's.

The neon sign is off, but the door is cracked open. I pause in the alley, comb my fingers through my hair and try not to think of the last time I showered. Maybe Randy will let me freshen up in the bathroom before he puts me on a pole.

A deep breath, and I walk through the dark doorway. A man sits on the stage, rifling through CDs. The strip club's namesake, ugly even in the silted shadows of his club. He's fat and balding, blunt fingers scratching his neck with a sandpaper sound.

But he's king here, and he knows it. He glances at me as I walk toward him and huffs in disgust. Hope dies, but I plant myself in front of him.

"I wanna dance."

"Thought I told you 'no' already." Randy goes back to sorting CDs. "Don't need a stripper with no tits."

"Put me on a pole and see what I can do." I'm bluffing. I've never danced naked in my life. But I know enough about how rough guys like their women. Growing up in a motorcycle club will teach a girl.

"Just told you. Don't need another dancer. Get your skinny ass outta here."

Fuck this. I stride away, detouring at the last second to the bathroom. Randy didn't even look at me.

Inside, I wash my face, take a good look and grimace. My skin is so pale it's almost translucent. There are ditches under my eyes. My backpack, my one possession, is filthy, spattered mud hiding the worse stains underneath. One glance, and Randy will know I spent last night curled in a doorway in a back alley—and that I'm desperate not to do it again. I look gross at best, or maybe hungover. My hands tremble a bit as I apply a little makeup. I'll wait in here until I feel less like a junkie, then go out and insist the proprietor of this fine establishment give me another chance. I'll grovel and do it sexy. I'll do what I have to—even suck Randy's dick.

By the time I've worked up the nerve to exit the bathroom, a deep voice fills the club. I slip from the bathroom but stay in the shadows.

Fat Randy has another petitioner.

"Just want you to hear me out." A big man spreads his hands. His broad shoulders block my view of Randy. The newcomer is big, but not with fat. From the solid way he fills out his flannel shirt and jeans, he's all muscle.

"No broad of mine is gonna up and leave to service a bunch of—"

"We'll pay. Room and board, ten thousand at the end of the season. More if she does a good job. My guys might tip."

I hug the wall, what I just heard reverberating through me. *Room and board and ten thousand dollars.*

"Eh," Randy grunts. "I'm not gonna let you poach my girls. They've got a good thing here and they know it. Summer's the busy season. They're not going to go to bumfuck nowhere and dance for a crew of dirty lumberjacks."

"I just thought—"

"The answer's 'fuck no.' Now get the fuck out. If I hear you're hanging around, talking to my girls about this, I'll have Bernie make sure you get the message. Bernie!" Randy shouts, and a tattooed hulk appears from the smoky gloom, plants his fists on the bar and leans forward like a gorilla.

Randy smirks. "Bernie doesn't talk much. He uses his fists instead, you get me?"

Shaking his head, the big guy pivots. I shrink into the shadows and watch his boots clomp past.

I get a quick look at his face—black beard clipped tight to a clenched jaw—before he hits the door with his hand and shoves it open. I'm following before I can stop myself.

"Hey, you," Randy sees me and shouts. "Get out of here. Don't need no more dancers." I leave before he calls a bouncer to toss out my 'skinny ass.'

I scurry up the sidewalk, chasing the big guy. "Hey!" I call but it comes out a raspy whisper. He keeps walking. He's got a nice stride, long and loose. Faded jeans, stained and washed clean. Boots and a thermal shirt under Carhartt plaid. He looks like a lumberjack, a rugged sort who grew up here with the pines.

Be brave.

"Excuse me." I get close enough to touch his elbow. He swings around and glowers at me, black brows knotted, beard hiding a frown. I try not to cringe.

"Um... did you say you were looking for a female entertainer?"

His eyes skip up and down my lean frame.

I raise my chin and puff out my chest a little. "I'm game."

He just looks at me. His jaw is square and hard under a bristling black beard.

"You work there?" He tilts his head toward Randy's neon sign.

"Not yet. I was going to apply, but I like your offer better."

LEE SAVINO

He looks away a moment, and I see him thinking of a way to blow me off.

"Where would I be staying?" I blurt.

"Logging camp about fifty miles north of here."

"I didn't realize there was anything north of this town," I try to joke.

"There isn't. The camp's remote. Nothing but bears, trees and us."

You're not a bear? I shut the teasing down. "And you just want a dancer? Not anything else?" A breeze kicks up and I shiver. The thought of taking off my clothes makes me cold.

He looks at me a for a second, his gaze distant like he's seeing right through me.

"Did you eat?" he grunts.

"What?"

"Breakfast." He jerks his head down the street at a diner. "My treat. We'll talk."

～

LINCOLN

THE GIRL SLIDES into the booth, visibly relaxing into the warmth. She's all skin and bones in tight jeans and a fucking hoodie. A hoodie, during this cold snap. She looks like she's barely outta high school.

When I first saw her out of the corner of my eye at Randy's, I clocked her as an addict, but her eyes and voice were clear and brave. It took courage to run after me, and I respect that.

I'll warm her up, buy her a good meal, give her some money to buy a decent jacket, and let her down easy.

She's biting her lip, shoulders hunched. Fuck, I don't want her afraid of me.

"How old are you?"

She licks her lips. "Twenty-one."

I can't keep from scoffing.

She meets my frown with a proud chin. "Here." She fumbles in the backpack she's been gripping like it's a safety blanket. Slaps down a plastic rectangle. ID.

Sierra Woodhouse. Organ donor. Motorcycle license, too, which is interesting. And yes, if I did my math correctly, she is twenty-one.

I relax a little. She looks like jailbait, but unless this is a forgery, she's not. I hate the thought of someone so young working at a place like Randy's. But I ain't paid to care. Everyone's got their own fucked up story. The best thing about living away from civilization is that I don't have to deal with people's bullshit anymore.

"Tell me about the job," she demands. Feisty. Stronger than she looks.

"Food first." I prop up my menu. Workman's special right at the top includes two of practically everything on the breakfast menu. They know how to feed men around here. I order the meal and coffee from the tired waitress and wait for Sierra. She's biting her lip, looking at the menu with an almost pained expression. Nothing hurts an empty stomach like a possible feast.

"Make that two coffees and two specials." I hand back my menu but take Sierra's and set it aside. "I'll let you know if we need more food."

Sierra keeps her gaze on the table, like trying to choose what to eat took the fight out of her. Her eyelashes are dark smudges against her pale skin. She has a few freckles.

"You from around here?" I ask.

"No. You?"

I sigh. "Wisconsin. Thought I was used to cold weather."

"And?"

"Hell isn't hot. Hell is cold and, November to May, it's right here."

"How far are we from the Arctic Circle?"

"Not far enough. There's just two seasons up here. Winter, and the one we're in now."

"What's the one we're in now?"

"Blackfly and mosquito season."

That gets a tiny smile.

I shut up until they put food in front of us and motion for her to dig in. She tries to be dainty, but she shovels the cheap calories in. I order a second cup of coffee and wait until she slows to talk.

"So, the job."

Her eyes flick up to mine. They're green and striking, slightly almond-shaped. Not one hundred percent Caucasian background then. Her face is decent enough, even pretty if it wasn't so thin and hollowed out, but her eyes are fucking gorgeous.

"I've got a crew of guys up in logging country. This is our busy season, and we don't have time for off days. I don't want my guys running down here to get a fix."

"By fix you mean 'pussy.'" She doesn't shy away from the word. "You want one on call."

I shrug. It seemed a good idea at the time. Now, I'm not so sure.

"What does the job entail? Like, how many hours?"

"You dance every night. Other than that, the time is yours. Eat with us, sleep in, do girly shit—"

"I'll do it."

I sit back with a sigh. The booth creaks. "Have you

stripped before?"

"No. But I've waitressed. And how hard is it to take off your clothes?"

I study her a moment. Her wrists are small with delicate blue veins. I could snap them with one hand.

"I don't look like much, but I'm tough," she continues. "I catch on quick. I'll be good for your guys, I swear."

"There's more. The guys might want... more."

"I can do that, too." She meets my stare head-on. I have to admit; my dick perks up a bit at her boldness.

"You have experience?" I ask, like this is a regular job interview.

"I'm not a virgin, if that's what you're asking. My momma told me about the birds and the bees."

I snort. She's blunt and honest. A breath of fresh air.

"So you'd be willing to..."

She shrugs. "I can do anything for that amount of money. Anything and anyone."

I stare at her. "You'd have to get tested. We'll pay for the doctor."

She hesitates a moment. "Okay."

Fuck, what can I say to deter her? "There are seven other guys, all built like me."

"I won't break. I can take you." Her green eyes bore into mine.

Now I'm sprung, my dick hard enough to punch through the table. "Fuck me," I mutter.

Her glare turns into a flinty smile. "That's my job."

I wave to the waitress. This was supposed to be easy. A pity meal. I'd peel off some bills and send her on her way. But now I'm not so sure she'll go.

"Give me a chance," she says. "I can do the job. Take care of me and I'll take care of you."

Rough voices outside and the diner door flies open. A crew of men stomp inside, talking loudly. Sierra practically shrinks into a ball as they pass. And I know.

She's on the run. She's hiding from someone. Fuck me, there's no way I can say 'no' now.

Maybe I can just bring her back for the night. I try to imagine what Saint will say when he sees her. He's even bigger than me.

"Did you spend the night here, in a motel?" she asks. "If you still have your room, I'd like to shower before we leave."

"Sure." Maybe I can slip out of the motel. Leave her some money and pay for the room a few nights. Stop at a church or something to get someone to check on her. Little thing like her shouldn't be alone.

As we step outside the diner, a motorcycle revs in the distance and Sierra ducks her head, darting closer to me.

A man definitely did her wrong. Maybe a few of them— out here motorcycle clubs own whole towns. In the MC world, men are men, and women are property. If a club member got hold of Sierra, they wouldn't think twice about beating the sass out of her. The thought makes me want to destroy something.

"This way." I step between her and the road, keeping her on the inside of the sidewalk in case a truck splashes by. Such a damn gentleman.

We're halfway to the motel when I realize I'm not shortening my stride. She's marched right along with me, head high. Not asking for anything.

Fuck, I like this girl.

"Here." I stop in front of a general store. "I need a few things." We enter and her eyes dart around. "Pick out some warmer clothes," I order. "I'll buy." In case she was tempted to steal the things she needs. "And any girly shit you might need—enough for a month." She can go to a safehouse fully stocked up.

I kill time until she appears at the register with a little cart filled with way too few things. Pink toiletries and a few thermals, another pair of jeans.

Muttering a curse, I grab a winter jacket that looks like it might be her size—or at least not make her look like she's wearing her mother's bathrobe. "Cold up in the boonies. Remember? Cold as Satan's heart." I toss the jacket in front of the cashier and add a few plaid shirts. "What's your shoe size?"

She tells the cashier, who heads off to grab what I instruct. Boots. No more soaked tennis shoes. As an afterthought, I add a few pairs of socks.

"I thought you'd want me in less clothes," she murmurs when the cashier is distracted. My dick jumps again.

I shake my head. "This way the show lasts longer." If I don't think of her body under all these clothes, I won't get a boner in the middle of the general store. I pay before Sierra has time to flinch over the total.

When I unlock the door to the motel, it's my turn to flinch. She deserves more than this faded place with stains on the carpet and the stale smell of cigarettes. In the dim light, her skin seems to glow.

"Take your time."

"I won't be long."

I put on the TV to mask the sound of the shower. If there was time to make my escape, this is it. But a cowardly ass way to do it.

I stare at the screen and try not to imagine Sierra getting naked just a few feet away, behind a flimsy door.

∽

Sierra

Fuck, hot water feels good. The heat sluices to my bones. A nice, clean feeling plus the food and I'm ready to live again. I wish I could linger, but I'd bet ten-thousand dollars Lincoln's gonna dump me as a charity case. He'll either walk out now or wait to drive me to a homeless shelter. Which means I've got to convince him I've got what it takes for this job, ASAP.

I wash and shampoo in record time. Once out and wrapped in a towel, I mop steam from the mirror and stare at my reflection. Black hair slicked back. Green eyes, too large for my narrow face.

It's now or never. But I have a secret weapon. After drawing it on, I open the door, pausing to pose in the doorway. I timed it right—Lincoln is still here, eyes blank on the TV screen.

He's a big man. Young, strong, good looking. He's got the world in the palm of his hand. But I've got the one thing he doesn't have. The one thing he needs. Pussy.

I let the towel drop.

Lincoln drags his eyes from the television and visibly starts.

"I think you should sample the goods before you take me home." I saunter over, letting him drink me in. I'm wearing an almost see-through thong and bra—my stripper outfit. They didn't sell anything sexy at the general store. Probably a good thing. Their idea of sexy underwear might be pink plaid.

I move in front of the TV and Lincoln isn't even tempted to take his eyes from me. Pretending the sports newscast is club music, I start to dance.

This is my show. I'm in charge, swaying in front of him, dipping and swiveling my hips. I'd watched the strippers do this, and the wannabe old ladies at the Hell Riders' clubhouse. His green eyes track my movements. He's holding his breath.

I may not be stripper material, but Lincoln's probably not been with a woman for a long time. Such a shame. The sharp planes of his face are perfect, even under the wild beard. His muscles are solid under my hands. A man like this should be worshipped by a woman, often.

I climb onto his lap and straddle him, knees on the bed, my legs stretched over his large thighs. His large hands immediately slide to my back, supporting me, but he makes no move to go further. No problem. I got this.

This close, Lincoln is a masterpiece, waiting to be enjoyed. I roll my body against his and let my hands explore the dormant power of his corded arms, his solid chest, his broad shoulders. He's rigid and strong everywhere I touch. I get lost in him.

Then I dip my head close to his face, angling my head to see how we'd fit if we kissed. My mouth hovers over his, my lips just out of reach. Our breath mingles.

A second later, he raises his chin, tipping his face up to meet mine. A slight move but it tells me all I need. I've got him under my spell. I rise up and turn, settling my ass on his lap and gyrating to a silent beat. I lie back like he's my armchair, my little body draped over his powerful frame, and grind his cock against my soft ass. It grows even larger. A monster.

I whirl again and unbutton his jeans deftly. Jack was often drunk or high when we bumped uglies—I have plenty of practice stripping down a man's jeans just enough to ride. Lincoln's abs flex as I slip a hand in and explore. Sweet

Jesus, he's a nice handful. I try but can't close my fingers around his thickness. My sex prickles as my body prepares to take him.

"Sierra—" he says. Before he can slow this down, I stop his mouth with mine. I practically attack him, throwing my whole body into the kiss. His thick cock twitches in one of my hands while my other clamps on his neck, holding his lips to mine. I press against him, pushing until he leans back with a groan. I free my hands long enough to unbutton his shirt and scooch up his thermal. I'm almost naked, it's his turn. I want to see what I'm dealing with. He helps me, whipping the shirt off. His arms fall around me, caging me but just holding me without applying pressure. He's panting, jaw flexing as if he's holding back something he wants to say.

He's giving me an out. I arch a brow and roll against him, lazy and inviting. My sex presses closer to his. I'm wet, slipping over the coarse hair around his heavy length. A few inches and he'll be inside me.

He reaches down the bed for something—his wallet. I cock a brow as he fingers the billfold, searching for something.

"Condom," he says. I nod, quickly removing my panties while watching solemnly as he sheathes himself. This is happening.

"Shh." I hush his unspoken doubts. "Let me take care of you." His hips thrust upwards, seeking me. It's too late to stop now. I lift up, point him toward my wet entrance, and drive down.

A groan escapes. I was right. It's been a long time for him. I wriggle a little, accepting his girth. It's tight, a little uncomfortable, but not as bad as it would be if I weren't so wet. I haven't had a man inside of me since Jack... but this isn't the time to think about Jack.

We rock slowly together, eyes wide open. It's a conversation between strangers. *Hello, how are you, is this what you like? How about if I touch you now? Here... or here? Tell me what you like.* Our hips align, move against each other in easy rhythm. Our bodies become fast friends.

I close my eyes and give over to sensation. There's a man under me again, but he's nothing like Jack. Jack was a grown-up boy, goofy and heroin thin. Lincoln is all man, his body solid and powerful under mine. He cups my bottom, covering the whole of it with his large hands. *You're safe now, with me. I'll protect you. No one gets through me to you.* I've known him a little over two hours, and I already heard the silent promise. I want to believe...

Flesh slaps against flesh. The conversation grows in intensity, the sentences curt. *Faster, harder. Now. Please.*

My orgasm strikes, flashing up my spine. I stiffen and fall against him. He groans and bucks into me, once, twice, and grinds into me, rooting deep. We fall together, a jumble of limbs on the cheap, rickety bed.

I rise first, pushing back my wet hair. Lincoln admires the flush on my chest and in my cheeks. I'm not a skinny-ass charity case anymore. I'm a fucking sex goddess, and he knows it.

A furrow appears between Lincoln's heavy brows as he regards me. I grin, wrinkling my nose a little as if to say, *didn't expect that, didja?*

No. His owlish gaze tells me. A muscle jerks in his jaw— an unwilling smile, then he gives in, rolling back his head and laughing, white teeth flashing against his dark beard. As the happy, carefree sound fills the room, I head to the bathroom, strutting like a salesman who has just closed the deal.

2

S ierra

LINCOLN'S TRUCK hits a pothole and I jerk awake. A good fuck, a shower, a hot meal on top of a long month being on the run—I didn't have a chance of staying awake. I barely remember turning onto the road leading out of town.

Sleep, whispers the heat blowing from the vents. *Safe,* say Lincoln's large hands on the steering wheel.

"Sorry," the man mutters, navigating the truck around muddy craters. The pavement is so bad, cracked and broken from icy winters, we might as well be off-road.

"It's okay," I sigh and close my eyes again. I haven't been this comfortable in over a month. Maybe longer. It's strange not to have fear gripping me. For weeks, fear has driven me forward, pushing me through the tough sleepless nights, the long bus rides clutching my backpack to me. I ate, drank, breathed it. It was my energy, muscles and bone, knitting me together. Now that we're turning onto a long logging road, it loosens its grip a little, but I still need it.

I did it. I got the job. I'm the new 'entertainer' for a crew of lusty lumberjacks. Eight men, strong and strapping as Paul Bunyan. Every night, seven days a week. I'll be getting it once a day, twice on Sundays.

Nausea clutches my stomach. I press my forehead to the cold car window, breathing in and out carefully.

"You all right?"

"Just carsick."

He reaches an arm across my seat and tweaks the manual crank to crack my window a little. Sweet. "We're almost home."

I nod, and angle my head into the flow of fresh air.

Lincoln's square jaw tenses for a mile before he says, "You don't have to... with all of us. It's your choice. I'm not going to let them hurt you."

"It's okay." He's trying to be nice, but there's no way half the guys are going to stand by while I bestow sexual favors on the other half. Lincoln will have a war on his hands, and he won't win. The victors will divide the spoils.

And I'm the spoils.

It'll be better than being a sweetbutt in a grungy MC clubhouse. At least this way, I'm getting paid.

We're quiet the rest of the way. The truck bounces over a few epic potholes before turning into a lot guarded by huge wire gates and a high wall around a muddy yard. Coiled barbed wire tops the wall—to keep people out or in?

Inside the walls, mud-spattered logging machines crouch like awkward insects. A few workers cluster around the back of one, turning as we roll past. A curious face framed by a bushy red beard pokes out from a truck cab, but I shrink back in the seat before he gets a good look at me.

Ahead is a long, low building with a few ATVs parked out front. Lincoln guides his vehicle to the end of the line, turns off the engine, palms the keys. I get a nasty jolt—Lincoln's truck is my only way out or in. I can hide here from the Riders, but not from the eight men who hold my next few months in their calloused hands. I swallow, my mouth suddenly dry. What have I done?

"Stay there. I'll get your door." Lincoln grabs his own duffel and the few plastic bags left over from our shopping trip at the general store.

I start to open my door anyway, just to feel like I have some control, and nearly hit a stocky, dark-haired dude prowling alongside the truck.

He scowls at me—tanned skin, dark eyes and plump lips too sensuous for his scraggly goatee—and keeps walking, shooting a nasty glare back my way before disappearing into the building.

Holy hell, they make lumberjacks pretty. Must be all the fresh air. Shave the pathetic beard, mousse the silky dark hair, power-wash the mud off him and he'd be ready for a GQ photo shoot. Those cheekbones! Shame he hides them under the facial hair.

"That's Mason," Lincoln says at my elbow and I jolt, my breath rattling through me. I duck my head and shake my hair over blushing cheeks, hiding my reaction to Mason's movie star good looks and gracefully muscled body.

"He doesn't like people. Don't mind him." Lincoln holds out a hand, and I take it before hopping down, christening my new boots in mud.

Mason, Mason, Mason, I chant as we head to the door. One of the eight. Too late to make a good first impression on him. Not that I can compete with the one he made on me.

Inside the building is a small mess hall—a long table

surrounded by eight chairs. Beyond the table, a hall leads to several closed doors. There's no sign of Mason.

Two guys drift from the hall. I give them a perky little wave. One nudges the other, mouthing, "Fresh meat." I step back, following Lincoln to the left, into a galley kitchen full of warmth and rattling pans. A massive guy with a shaved head and midnight skin mans the stove, stirring the contents of a pot big enough to fit me.

"Any luck?" he asks, and Lincoln steps aside to reveal me.

"Hi." The word dies in my throat as the big guy looks me up and down and back to his bubbling stew without changing expression.

"Saint, this is Sierra," Lincoln tells him. "She'll be staying with us for awhile."

"Didn't realize we were a hotel." The big guy, Saint, lifts the ladle and tastes the broth, pours it back in. With a hand five time the size of mine, he adds a pinch of spice. his face still wiped of expression.

"She'll earn her keep. Just like you. Like all of us." Lincoln glares at the huge guy as if daring him to argue. Ballsy move. I don't think I'd bet against the big guy in a fist-fight. He's roughly the size of the commercial fridge in the corner.

Shrugging, Saint turns his back on us.

"Come on." Lincoln guides me out of the kitchen. Strike two. My knuckles go white on my bag's strap, and I force a smile on my face as we head back to face the rest of the guys. I can't afford a third strike.

Men pour into the main room from each entrance. Big, bearded guys, forming a towering forest around me. I lean against the table and let my bag tumble from weary arms. I hope dinner is soon. These guys look at me like they're hungry and I'm their meal.

Three of them tromp in from the outside. More big guys, big as the door, with muscles made from spending the day tearing trees up by the roots and snapping them in half over their knees. Or whatever lumberjacks do.

They tromp in and surround me, tall as trees, their cut off sleeves showing biceps resembling corded wood. Lincoln wasn't lying when he said the crew were all guys like him. I'm lost in the woods.

"Who's this?" one asks. A redhead. On the other side of me, an identical redhead—so identical to the first I'm sure one's a reflection from some mirror—extends a finger to trace the edge of my hood. The scent of the outdoors washes over me, fresh and clean and bracing. I shrink in my clothes.

"Hey," Lincoln snaps at the newcomers. "Wipe your boots."

"Awww, Mom," the redhead whines. He trudges back with his silent doppelganger, and I can breathe again.

Meanwhile, one of the guys from the hall, tall with dirty blond Kurt Cobain locks, comes closer. His tattooed arms add sleeves to his white wife beater.

"Hi," I say, extending my hand. "I'm Sierra."

"Sierra," he drawls, and bypasses the handshake, pulling me into a hug, bringing me eye level with a skull tattoo. There's a snake coming out of one eye socket; it writhes as his bicep flexes. "I'm Jagger."

"Jagger," Lincoln says. "Sierra agreed to come stay with us for the season."

"Mmmm," Jagger clutches me closer. He must have a hammer in his pocket, because the handle is poking me in the leg. Either that, or he knows exactly why I'm here.

"That's enough," Lincoln clips. "She just got here, hasn't even met everybody. Give her some space."

"Of course," Jagger says, but keeps an arm hooked around my neck. Not big on personal space, is Jagger. "Make your introductions. I'll help. That's Roy and Tommy." He points to two guys and turns me before I get a good look at their faces. "And these are the twins."

The two redheads by the door straighten and I blink, seeing double.

"Elon and Oren." Jagger's finger points at the space between them. "Irish dad, Jewish mother. Are they're circumcised? I guess you'll find out."

He tries to tug me around again, but I keep staring at the identical ginger twins. There has to be a way to tell them apart.

One has a small mole near his right eye, above his beard. "What are your names again?" I ask, and when the guy with the mole points to himself and tells me shyly, I memorize it. *Oren.* Doesn't matter if he's the mirror image of his brother. He's one of the eight, and I'm going to make a good impression.

"You're staying?" Elon asks. His stark blue eyes are framed by extra long lashes.

"Yep. Isn't she cute? She's so little," says Jagger, who was standing behind the door when God passed out tact.

"Don't worry, there's plenty of me to go around," I say to the assembly.

"Huh," someone grunts from the direction of the kitchen. Saint.

"She'll do." Jagger grins like he owns me. Keeping his arm around my shoulders, he picks up my backpack. "I'll show you to your room."

"Me too," both the twins chime together.

"Nope." Saint points a spatula at one of them. "KP duty."

"You're cooking tonight?" Jagger asks the big man.

"Yep. Gumbo."

"Awesome. Get some meat on her bones." Jagger hugs me to his side again and I roll my eyes. I duck out of his hold, straightening just as Lincoln says to one of the twins, "She can dance tonight, but nothing more. Not until she sees the doctor."

I gulp back my retort, grateful for the one night reprieve. Judging by the horny looks I'm getting from the twins and Jagger, I'm not going to have a night off for a while. There's eight guys here and I'm the only woman around for miles.

Just then Mason stomps past, glaring like I'm mud under his boots.

Scratch that. Mason probably won't touch me if I paid him.

Jagger throws his arm around me again and his erection manages to poke me in the thigh. I'll probably get it twice on his night.

I shake Roy and Tommy's hands—nice guys, too polite to leer—and sneak another peek at Mason. He says something to Saint, and runs his hand through his shock of raven black hair. Shadows fall on the hollows under his cheekbones. It's impossible. It's CGI, or madly contoured makeup. No man should be this gorgeous.

But he is. And he's looking my way like he hates me.

"Mason, meet..." Jagger's voice dies as Mason shoulders roughly past him, heading out of the room. We all watch his retreating back.

I find my voice. "Who peed in his Cheerios?"

Oren chokes and Jagger giggles. I've never heard a man giggle until now.

"Mason hates women," Jagger tells me.

"That's okay." I cross my arms over my small chest. "He doesn't have to like me to get his dick sucked."

"Ah, Sierra, fresh as the mountain air." Jagger smiles like a proud papa. "Let's finish the tour."

The tour consists of Jagger dragging me from room to room, with Elon following us like a puppy.

"This is the mess hall. And that's the entertainment center." He points to a couple of loungers and a couch set up in front of a giant TV. "We don't get many channels, so there's not too much entertainment. But I guess that's why we've got you." Jagger cocks his head at me, and I meet his gaze blandly. If he's not embarrassed about what I'm here for, then I'm not going to be either.

"That's me," I quip. "Your own personal sex toy."

Poor Elon blushes to his red roots. The way he and his brother blush and stare, I wonder if they're virgins. Maybe just super inexperienced.

"This way are some of the bedrooms." Jagger leads me down a long hall. The building is L-shaped, with the kitchen and main door at the elbow. "And..." He throws open a door to a dorm-style bathroom, multiple urinals and shower stalls all in a row.

"Nice, isn't it?" Jagger says proudly. "Most camps have bathrooms and showers in a separate building, like a camp-ground. But Lincoln had the company build it to his specifi-cations. The company wanted him as lead," Jagger explains. He continues down the hall, pointing out the individual doors. "Usually there are just barracks, but we've got bedrooms. More privacy." He swings open one of the doors, smirking. "This room's mine."

"Great," I murmur. There's clothes and stuff strewn all over the dark space. Hovering over everything is the telltale musk of marijuana, confirming my suspicions: Jagger is the lumberjack equivalent of a college stoner.

The door opposite Jagger's is half open. Roy and Tommy pause mid-conversation to give me polite but guarded smiles. I nod to them and turn to my guides.

"Where's my bedroom?"

"Other wing. But my door's always open." Jagger lopes back the way we came.

My room is on the far end of the second hall. A twin bed, concrete floor, a battered dresser. All the charm of an empty dorm room.

"Cozy." My voice echoes a little. Jagger puts my bag on the bed. Elon fetches sheets and a blanket—more faded plaid—and I thank him. I sit down on the bed and bounce, testing the springs. Not that it matters. It's way more comfortable than a doorway in an alley.

"You want to hang out now, or nap or something?" Jagger asks, hovering over me.

"Nap," I say decisively. He looks disappointed but leaves without protest, shutting the door quietly.

I close my eyes and sag back on the bed. Despite the nap in the car, I could sleep another hundred years. At least my stomach isn't flopping like a fish. The mysterious illness seems to have been cured by food.

I doze a moment before wrenching myself up. Just because I met the guys doesn't mean my first day on the job is over. Lincoln is sold, Jagger and the twins obviously want to fuck me, but Mason definitely doesn't. Saint, Tommy and Roy also looked ambivalent. Fifty percent chance of keeping this gig, and I don't like those odds.

I'm almost safe, a hundred miles away from the Hell Riders' territory. A hundred miles away from everything. I can't go back now. My bones ache with the thought of running another step.

I have to keep this job.

After running a brush through my hair and straightening my clothes, I head back to the common room. Voices echo down the hall, loud and male.

Mason stands in front of Lincoln, his arms outspread. Even if I couldn't hear the argument, I could tell from Lincoln's tight jaw that he's getting shit.

"This is fucked," Mason spits. "I know you wanted a woman, but her? She belongs in a halfway house. Pussy's probably so full of disease—"

"If you want to talk about me behind my back," I let my voice ring out, "make sure I've left the room."

Mason stiffens like I've touched him. "We don't need a junkie whore."

"I'm not a whore. Whores get paid."

"You're not getting paid?" Jagger's brow wrinkles.

"I'm getting paid to dance," I emphasize. "I'm putting out for free." I turn to Mason and continue coolly, "Get on my bad side and you won't get any." I glance at Lincoln to see if he'll back me up.

He nods. "That's right. Paying for sex is illegal. But anything that happens after the dance is between consenting adults."

"Don't worry," I say to Jagger, who looks like someone cancelled Christmas. "I plan on distributing favors equally. I like men, and I like sex."

Mason opens his mouth but Saint lumbers past him to the table, sets something down and motions me over. He pulls out a chair and I sit automatically.

"You're too thin," he rumbles.

Don't worry, big boy, I can take you. I start to say when the steam from the bowl of goodness hits my nose. My mouth fills with saliva and my stomach almost lurches out of my gut.

Saint thumps a spoon down beside my hand. "Eat," he orders.

He doesn't have to say it again. I shovel food in my mouth, not only because I'm hungry, but because Saint looms behind me with his arms crossed over his chest, glaring at everyone and no one.

"I fed her breakfast," Lincoln defends himself.

"I have a fast metabolism," I mumble with my mouth full. "Damn, this is good." The broth is just a touch spicy, there's sausage and vegetables and rice. I'd sell my body for this, oh yes I would.

"Eat more." Saint rests his hand on the back of my neck —just for a moment, but there's care in his touch.

"Wow," Jagger says when Saint disappears back into the kitchen. "He likes you."

"'Cause he fed me?"

"That and he didn't pick you up and throw you out," Lincoln says thoughtfully. Mason grunts and stomps back to his bedroom.

"You know why they call him Saint?" Jagger says. "He played football in college in Louisiana. Rumor is he was a top pick to go pro, but he finished his degree and came north instead. Fastest bucker around. Makes gumbo when he's in a good mood, and if we're lucky, he'll share it."

"And you?" I ask. "Is your name really Jagger?"

"I got moves."

I roll my eyes.

"Seriously. I'll dance with you if you want."

"I'll think about it." We talk music as the room fills.

More of the guys join us and despite Jagger making it

sound like Saint is stingy with the product of his culinary genius, the big guy ladles generous gumbo portions onto their plates. Oren serves up plates of biscuits. I watch with wide eyes as each guy eats about twenty each. Both Lincoln and Elon sacrifice from their pile to put a few on my plate, and they just look at me when I protest that I'm full.

By the end of the meal, I'm comfortable around the big guys. For the most part they treat me like a friend, or their best friend's little sister. Jagger shares his Coke and I get in a burping contest with him. Even Saint joins in. Everyone except Mason, who wears his permanent expression of disgust.

"I've got an idea," he purrs, dark eyes on me. He's balanced on the back legs of his chair. "Why doesn't Sierra give us a show? Just a little taste of what we're buying," he adds, before Lincoln can remind him I don't start work until after the doctor's appointment.

The guys start to protest that I just got here and I hold up a hand. "I gotta warn you, I'm really full. I have a food baby." I pat my stomach.

"That's hot," Jagger mutters.

"But I think it's a great idea, Mason," I say sweetly. "Just let me get changed."

As I walk past him, I give his chair a little push. To keep his balance he has to set the front legs down hard. I hide my grin. Pissing Mason off is my new favorite hobby.

Behind the closed door of my bedroom, I rub my face and will my heartbeat to settle. This is happening. I'm gonna strut out there in my skivvies and give them a show. This is what I signed up for, and I'm not gonna back out now.

I just have to ace the group interview. I'm not naive enough to think that Mason still couldn't convince the guys to send me back. So I have to show my stuff, and make sure it's the best thing they've ever seen.

I'm the only woman around for miles. How hard can it be?

When I re-enter the group room, every guy swivels to watch. Underneath the table, there are quite a few tents in the faded work pants. *Pretty fuckin' hard. But that's how I like it.*

Some joker turned the lights down except for one that shines like a spotlight on a space besides the table, far enough so everyone can see me. I stop in the center of the makeshift stage and smooth my hands down the tails of my shirt.

It's now or never.

I got this.

I point to Jagger and he turns on the music. *Into You* by Ariana Grande. Good song. I roll my shoulders back, close my eyes and start swaying to the music. My fingers play with the buttons of my new shirt. I'm wearing Carhartt plaid over my best bra and panties, and nothing else. My little lumber-jack-themed stripper outfit. I'm only missing a pair of Timberland boots.

Unbuttoning my shirt, I let my hips swing, twitching and dipping to the beat, giving the guys little glimpses of my skin under the red plaid. The chorus comes on and I toss my head back, peeling off the shirt and waving it around my head before tossing at Mason. He catches it before it hits him in the face. Nimble fucker.

I strut over to the table, my eyes on Lincoln. He watches me warily as I grab his shoulders, straddle his lap, stick my barely clad boobs in his face and gyrate. Around us, the guys hoot. My smile stretches my face and Lincoln relaxes, his hands sliding up my back. I grab a biscuit, put it in my mouth, and scissor up to offer it to him. He snaps at it but I jerk away at the last minute, shaking my head. I bounce in his lap as I eat the whole thing, stuffing my cheeks like a chipmunk and licking honey butter off my fingers.

By the time I'm done, Lincoln looks like he's a second away from sweeping the dishes off the table and laying me there as his feast. Perfect.

I ooze off him and skate by the twins, letting my fingers trail along their necks. Their heads turn like owls as I sashay past Roy, pausing to writhe my body between him and Tommy. I dance over to Jagger and his arms open to welcome me. At the last minute, I flip around and lean back into his hard torso. I twerk into his crotch as he crows—I knew he'd like this.

Around the table, all eyes are on me. Even Mason's, who's balanced on his chair's back legs again, arms crossed, jaw clenched, shadows pooling on the hard planes of his face.

Smiling, I leave Jagger's clinging arms, stepping from his lap onto the table. I toss my head and dance my heart out, my hips hitting the beat hard, my shoulders swiveling. I step carefully to a bare spot in front of Saint and crouch down, then crawl like a panther toward him. His eyes glint in his stone mask. I know just what to do to make his expression crack. I lean back on my arms, plant my feet wide, and rock my hips back and forth, waving my pussy in front of his face. I flip off the table and lean over it, sticking my tailbone in the air and swaying my ass in Saint's direction. I pretend to spank myself until he breaks position. His huge hand covers my small butt-cheek. Chuckling to myself, I twist and dance away, shaking my finger at him. There's no mistaking the hunger in his eyes now. I wink at him, my pout promising plenty of opportunity to spank me later.

Everywhere I look, I'm met with the same glorious horny gaze. Even Mason doesn't bother to hide it. Jagger tries to grab me as I moonwalk by.

I've done it. They all want to fuck me. And they can't. *Nu uh*, my wagging finger says. I lick it and circle one pointy nipple until my body screams, *It'll be worth the wait.*

The song is ending. Time for the big finish.

I grab my chair and drag it near the light. Sit with my knees on either side of the seat. My crotch on display, I stick my hands in my see-through panties and rub, closing my eyes and smiling to myself, imagining how jaws have hit the floor. The song switches over to *Candy Shop* by 50 Cent and Olivia and I fondle myself in front of my audience, shivering with pleasure. I writhe on the chair like it's a lover. Ride it like a rodeo bronc while eight guys fuck me with their eyes. I've never done anything like this before. Not that I'm sheltered—I grew up around girls putting out for their biker of the month. It wasn't a party if a half-naked woman wasn't getting felt up in the corner, drinking a beer and giggling until the guy dragged her to one of the private rooms. Or peeled down her Daisy Dukes and boned her in front of everyone. When I started dating Jack, I made him claim a room for us before we did more than heavy petting. I never thought I could get off with an audience.

I was wrong.

Lightning sizzles under my fingers and I arch my body into an exaggerated bow. I'm so close. So close. But for some reason, I want to savor this moment. Dance on the edge.

As the song wraps up, I pull my fingers out of my panties and lick them clean. I'm a hot little number. Oh yeah.

Without a backward glance, I rise and strut back to my room.

"That's all for now," I call over my shoulder. "Night night, boys."

There's a clatter of chairs. I'd bet a grand half the guys go right to their rooms—or the shower.

I close the door to my room and lean against it, shaking. I did it. There's no way they'll get rid of me. Not even Mason will push for it now.

I curl up on my new bed and pass out like I got fucked eight times.

SAINT

LINCOLN'S DOOR shakes as I approach. When I want, I can walk lightly enough to pass like the Angel of Death over the homes of the Israelites. Tonight, I want to give warning.

Lincoln sits on his bed, hands dangling between his knees, staring at nothing.

I stop in the open doorway and wait until he looks up. My shadow stretches to cover the tips of his boots, so it doesn't take long.

"Saint." He gives me a rueful smile and runs his hand through his hair.

"We need to talk." If I want, I can make my voice light and smooth, a Barry White timbre that flows like warm honey. Or I can hit the lower reaches of my register, the gravel rumble of an oncoming avalanche. Tonight, I want his bones to shake.

"Yeah." Lincoln passes hand over his face and stands. "Yeah, we do." He knows what he did. He knows he's earned this talk and he's willing to take it.

"What the fuck were you thinking?" Every other word has the weight of a punch. Lincoln winces. I lean into his room, but don't enter and don't shut the door. If I wanted, I could make Lincoln follow me somewhere we can talk privately. Tonight, I want all the guys to hear.

"I think it'll work out."

"She looks like she's got one foot in the grave."

"She was hungry and cold and alone. Caught me outside the strip club. She had been begging Randy for a job so she could eat." He spreads his hands and his voice rises. "What was I going to do?"

"Drive her to a shelter. Give her some money. This isn't a halfway house."

"She was one second away from offering herself to any trucker walking the streets. I thought it would be better to bring her back here." He raises his chin. "I think she can do the job."

"This isn't what we agreed to." I fight to keep my voice level. "We discussed this. We need a woman who can take us." I could see her in my mind's eye, the type of woman I'd choose. A painted jade, made of makeup and plastic, who could play a part. A woman who'd chosen the role long ago. A cum doll in a candy-coated shell, choosing johns who can pay for her next boob job or coke habit. Not a girl, trying so hard to be brave. Not an innocent with no armor. Not Sierra, pale and lissome and wholesome as a dairy maid, with nothing to defend herself but brash wit and sheer stubbornness. "This kid can't do what's necessary."

Lincoln shakes his head, his breath hissing out. "I thought so too, and then I spent some time with her. You gotta get to know her, Saint. She's... her will is strong.

"Her will is strong," I repeat with heavy sarcasm. "Fuck. You fucked her."

With another shake of his head, Lincoln starts to turn away.

"You fucking fuck." My fingers catch the edge of his shirt. "You took advantage of her."

"Fuck I did,' Lincoln snaps around. He wades forward, crowding me until we're chest to chest and glaring, two seconds away from beating the shit outta each other. Big guy, Lincoln. Tall, good fighter. Any other guy facing him would shake in their boots. Not me.

"I fed her," he snarls in my face. "I got clothes for her, stuff she needed. I protected her." His eye slides to the side catching on a memory. "She's in trouble. Running from something."

"No shit. So you brought home a stray." My tone tells him just how stupid I think he is.

"Sierra isn't a stray. You saw her tonight."

Without permission, my thoughts snap to the dance. The pool of white light, Sierra's small body twitching as she brought herself to the brink of orgasm in front of us. I wanted to go to her, kneel down and finish her. Feel her warmth on my fingers and taste her sweetness.

"Yes," I say slowly. "That was something."

"She was magnificent. Admit it. After that performance, you really gonna look at me and tell me to send her back?"

Despite myself, my right hand curls. Not into a fist to beat some sense into Lincoln, but as if I've caught hold of a ghost, a slight, dancing angel, and I want to hang on and see if I can catch her. Keep her.

Fuck. I want Sierra.

"Saint?"

"One week," I say. "She has one week to prove herself. Then we send her back."

Sierra

MY CLIT WAKES ME. Swollen and angry, it pulses, reminding me that I fell asleep before rubbing one out. It wants me to finish what I started in the main room. After stroking myself for a few minutes, I sit up and head down the hall.

The door next to mine is open and I peek in as I pass. Two red heads swivel my way. Twin blue-eyed owls.

"Lincoln?" I ask, and Oren points down the hall.

"Last door on the right," Elon says. With a wink, I thank him and tiptoe to Lincoln's room. A brief knock, and I enter without permission.

The big guy sets aside a worn paperback, frowning as I slip to his side.

"I don't want to sleep alone," I snuggle next to him under the blanket.

He shifts to make room but it's no good. I have to plaster myself against him to fit next to his large body in the narrow bed. "You need to rest."

I let out a huge sigh.

"Don't worry"—his fingers play with the lines on my forehead—"they already like you."

I snort. "Mason doesn't."

"Mason doesn't like anyone."

We lie side by side, edges glued together. I hinge toward him.

"I'm horny."

It's his turn to sigh. "You don't want to save it? You might get tired of entertaining us." His fingers slide down my arm.

"No." I slip a leg over one of his. "I need it."

He rolls his heavy body over me, blocking out the light. I smile into his soft shirt, my breath stuttering as his biceps frame my head. He grabs a condom and this time I do the honors, rolling it on his throbbing length as his chest rises and falls more rapidly. A strong woodsy scent rises around us, tart pine and dry sawdust. I'm drunk on eau de lumberjack by the time I guide his dick inside. With a quiet gasp, he slides the rest of the way. His body glides over mine, muscles flexing on the edge of my vision, the granite plane of his lower abs dragging over mine, catching my clit. I hitch a calf over a jutting hip, pressing up for more friction, but other than that, I let him do the work. Tipping my head, I rub against the coarse fur of his chest, and let my fingers follow the happy trail all the way down. His movements speed and my mind turns to jelly.

"Jagger will say you broke your own rule," I murmur after, lazily stroking the firm contours of his back. Lincoln: strong as an oak, with thick dark hair like the pelt of an animal and a rich pine scent.

"Jagger can deal. Now be quiet," he says, not unkindly. "You need to rest up while you can."

But I want to lie here awake beside this tall tree of the man who made me safe, and drink in every second.

My eyelids flutter and close without my permission.

"Who are you running from?" Lincoln murmurs. But it's too late, I'm far away, under the spell of his rumbling voice, slipping into sleep.

3

S ierra

"Is it dangerous? The work?" I ask at my next meal. Lunch for the guys, breakfast for me. I slept clean through the morning and woke to Lincoln returning in a blast of outdoor air, still wearing a yellow helmet from his early shift. When he removes his headgear, his temples are silky with sweat.

Lincoln shrugs. "Can be."

"Lincoln's the safest crew chief in the territory," Jagger tells me around a mouthful of chili. "Maybe the country."

I raise my brows and study the leader over the rim of my coffee mug.

"You done?" he asks and when I nod, he rises and heads for the door. "Let's go."

"Where are you going?" Elon twists in his chair, red

brows knitting on his freckled forehead. Beside him, his brother does the same with an identical expression.

"Doctor," Lincoln answers for me.

"I'm not sick," I remind them, even as my stomach lurches with the uneven ratio of coffee to good food. I was queasy this morning but eating helped. In a few days I should be used to feeling full. "Health check-up. Don't wait up." I give the matching redheads a friendly wave, and nearly slam into Mason. He practically plows me over, heading toward the coffee pot with a muttered, "Watch it."

Still no love lost between me and him, but no need to start a real fight. I bite my tongue and scurry outside.

"You and Mason all right?" Lincoln asks as I vault into his truck. Last time I was in here, I was exhausted and one meal away from starvation. What a difference a day makes.

"Oh yeah. Sticks and stones." I hang on as Lincoln maneuvers around the worst of the potholes in the road and hide my grin. Boys throw stones at girls they like. "He can't hurt me. I'll give him a few days to warm up. I figured I'd dance for everyone, and pick a different guy each night to entertain... privately."

A thick lock of his hair falls across his brows as he nods. I stroke it back. He stills under my tender touch but keeps his broad hands on the wheel. I'm feeling lots of gratitude toward my very own Paul Bunyan. Last night was the best sleep I've had in years.

I wonder how he feels about sharing me with seven other guys.

In a carefully bland voice I tell him, "I can start with Jagger, then the twins, Roy and Tommy—"

"Roy and Tommy probably won't want anything but watching you dance."

"Really?"

He shrugs. "You can ask them, but I think they'll just want a dance."

"Lap dance?"

More shrugging.

"Okay. I'll ask them." Two less guys means I can fit everyone in one week. "After the twins I can do Saint, then Mason, then you." I watch his hands carefully, but they don't clench on the steering wheel. He seems perfectly happy to have me pass my favors around. "What do you think?"

"Sounds good."

"Anything I should watch out for? Other than Mason."

A moment of hesitation, and he says ruefully, "Saint. He thinks you're too small."

I rub my belly where a full meal is finally starting to settle. "I am small. But I'll fit him just fine. I fit you."

Lincoln snorts.

"Oh, come on. Are you saying he's bigger than you?" I ask with a sly glance.

"I'm not admitting that."

"Women have babies all the time. It can't be bigger than a baby's head." He shakes his head and I laugh. "I'm serious! My body is built for it."

"I don't want to think about someone as little as you having babies."

"That's why we're going to the doctor." I settle back in my seat as he turns onto the empty two-lane road that passes for a highway. After a few miles I say, "I can handle Saint. I bet I could handle both of you." I smile at his snort, and make note of the interested gleam in his eye.

~

MASON

"TIMBER!"

A CREAK, and the long silent moment—the forest's vigil for a falling giant. The trunk crashes to the ground with a spray of dirt. Elon, Roy, Tommy and I all pause, then march forward, leaves and downed branches crunching under my boots.

Chains clink. An engine grumbles in the distance. Overhead, birds shriek and fly and settle back on the branches like dust. Sawdust pyramids in tawny piles like snow.

"Mason," someone calls. Jagger. He's laughing like a chick, holding his chainsaw in front of him like a giant metal boner.

I turn away, because the joke wasn't funny the first time.

"So," the forest clown says, parking himself unwanted in the space beside me. "You gonna take your turn?"

I grunt.

"I'll take your night if you want. Sucks that she looks just like Anita."

I wait, but there's none of the usual burn in my chest at my ex-girlfriend's name.

"You were gonna marry her, right?"

"Right." If she had waited for me. If she hadn't fallen into bed with the first guy who looked like me.

It didn't mean anything. I knew as she told me, she didn't mean it to go so far. She only meant to make me jealous. Sometimes the things you don't mean bear the heaviest consequences. Sometimes the things you don't mean outweigh all the rest. Life's funny like that.

Come back. We can make it work.

When we'd made plans to have kids, I didn't think she'd get started without me.

The next tree twists as it falls, a final, graceful ballet. Tommy and I attach chains to the shorn trunk and signal to Oren in the truck at the base of the hill. Another thing of beauty brought down, humiliated, dragged through the mud. Grown so tall only to be cut down.

Yesterday, the ghost of Anita sat in the passenger's seat of Lincoln's truck. Today she'll put down roots. Soft hands, soft body, soft voice, binding chains to bring us down.

Or not. She's not Anita. I should remember that.

My saw bites into a lichened trunk with a spray of dust. A small slice can bring down a giant. I cry a warning and Tommy paces backwards as the massive deciduous floats down, knocking into a second one and sending it flying to the forest floor with a rain of leaves and broken branches.

My heart says: *Remember this. Don't get too close. You won't survive the fall.*

My dick says: *Worth it.*

My mind says: *Never again.*

In the place where the tree stood a minute ago, the sun streams in. Thick and golden for late afternoon. I pull off my helmet and swipe at sweat.

Jagger shouts something from the bottom of the hill. Tommy turns to answer.

Roy tromps through the brush beside me. "What's going on?"

Oren cups his hands around his mouth to call, "We're ending early tonight. More time with Sierra."

I close my eyes and imagine her. Sierra. A pale scrap of a person, lean with survival. Fine-boned beauty, fragile as a bird. She's done nothing to deserve the punishment I'll wreak upon her body.

I shouldn't take my anger out on her. It's not fair.

My woman—no, my ex woman—is carrying my brother's child. Life's not fair.

It should've been yours, Mason, she said. No regret or apology. Just accusation. It was my fault we fought all the time. My fault I announced we were on break and left. My fault I fell in love with the forest, my mistress. My fault my woman fell into another man's bed.

The sun's in the forest now. A break in the canopy. I pick my way across the new clearing, shielding my eyes from the falling coins of light.

I stand in the golden spotlight and spin in a slow circle, at the center of the ugly gashes left on the earth. The destruction satisfies the bitter part of me. Here, in a desolate place, I made my mark.

The pines wait on the edge, ready to grow in the gaps. Stringy saplings choked from the light. Until now.

Sometimes, good things die so the rest will thrive.

When I clench my fist, a lightning bolt jumps in the corner of my eye. I filled my skin with tattoos, a nice complement to the scars hidden on my soul. Someday a woman might ask for the story written on my body. Someday I'll meet someone who deserves to know.

Until then, I have Sierra. A warm body for me to wreak my revenge. She'll take my hate and my cum and when it's done, she'll be a used tissue to crumple and throw away. No feeling. No remorse.

"Soups on." Tommy pulls off his helmet. "Coming?"

"In a minute."

I crouch and pull out the picture from my back pocket. If the guys saw this they'd think I grew a pussy. Anita's face, just to the right of a tear. The rest of the picture bears my face. That ripped off portion is already in the trash.

I study Anita's golden beauty and wait for the knife in my chest. Nothing. I feel nothing. Anita's face used to be a golden blade made to carve up my insides. But the edge is dulled, along with the pain.

Anita's with my brother now. He'll make her happy. She is his.

Sierra is mine.

I leave the broken photo on the log. Above it, a few splinters stick up, the longest finger in the middle, the tree's final salute.

∼

Sierra

BLOOD. *In the dark, the liquid is the color of night, spreading over the bed. The human body has so much blood. I press cold flesh as if I can put some of it back.*

My ears ring from the gun blast, my voice coming from far away. "Jack? Jack?"

A rumble of voices, of motorcycle pipes. I run to the bathroom and dry-heave into the sink. It already smells like puke from the last time I was here. A lifetime ago. When I raise my head to the mirror, empty eyes stare back at me.

"Jack," I whisper. Too late. Jack is dead.

It's my fault.

Boots stomp in the hall and I back away, leaving red hand-prints beside the sink. I shrink into the tub, press bloodstained hands to my mouth to keep from screaming. Curses echo through the house. The roar of motorcycle pipes rip the air. More men bang the door, coming inside. The house is full of men, cursing and telling each other what I already know. Jack is dead, shot in the chest, bled out on the bed.

"Where's his bitch? The scrawny one—" Footsteps by the bathroom door. I shrink under the faucet, tiny enough to fit behind the scrunched shower curtain. Tiny enough to hide.

"Fucking bitch. She did this—"

"We'll find her. Bitch can't run far—"

The voices recede. I rise up, a ghost in bloody clothes. My red hands scrabble at the half-open window. I wedge my foot in the corner and find another foothold on the soap dish, just enough of a ledge to push up and wriggle through the window crack.

I stagger as I hit the ground. The front yard is full of bikes and angry men. Hugging the wall, I inch to the backyard, where coals still glow in the fire pit. My backpack sits next to a litter of empty beer bottles where I left it an hour, a lifetime, ago. The last time I touched it, Jack was alive. Now my hands are stained with his blood.

I grab my backpack and run into the night.

"Sierra?"

I jerk awake, turn wide eyes to Lincoln. He's frowning, reaching a hand to brush my hair back from my forehead. He looks like he's gonna ask me something but all he says is. "We're almost to the doctor."

I sit up, rubbing my face to wipe away the cold sweat. If only I could swipe away my nightmares so easily.

Tired little strip malls roll by. This town is bigger than the one Lincoln picked me up in, but not by much. A department store sign catches my eye. "Do we have time to stop?"

"We have a few minutes."

He drops me off and I grab what I need quick, heading to the registers just as he walks in. Heat flares in his eyes when he sees what I'm buying. Just like our first shopping excursion, he insists on paying. The cashier coos and smiles at us like we're newlyweds.

"How often do you go to town?" I ask once we're back in the car.

"Once a week or less, to pick up supplies. Usually Saint goes. He does the orders." His large hand strays to my knee as we idle at the light. He squeezes, gently. "If you need anything, come to me."

At the doctor's, I sit in the examination room, naked under a papery cover, kicking my feet like I'm twelve. I feel invincible—or at least healthy enough to pass a physical. Amazing what a proper amount of food does to the mood.

I sit, stand, offer my arm for a blood pressure cuff, go into the tiny bathroom to pee in a cup—everything the nurse tells me to do.

I'm already gaining weight, mostly in my breasts. I give them a pleased pinch and wince. My nipples are tender. I must be close to my period. I haven't gotten it in a while—a side effect of not eating enough.

The doc, a kindly old sort who's probably served this small town for a hundred years, enters and I sit up straighter. Time for the big exam. I know I'm gonna pass. I'm getting a birth control prescription and a paper saying I'm clean. I'll ask the doctor to sign in triplicate so Mason doesn't think it's a forgery.

"If you'll just put your feet here"—the doc motions to the stirrups—"and scoot down to the edge of the table."

I do as he asks, flushing at the vulnerable position. There's a stain on the ceiling tile that looks like the Hudson Bay. I keep my eyes on it as I answer questions about my sexual history. It doesn't take long. I was a virgin before Jack, and he didn't have many partners before me. We skipped a condom a few drunken times, but were pretty careful.

The clock on the wall clicks closer to 4:00 pm. In a few hours, I'll be back on my back with my legs wide, and getting paid for it. Oops, don't think about that. Don't want the doctor thinking he got me excited.

"All right." He snaps on gloves. "I'll have a look-see here. Make sure you're healthy and then check out the baby." He gives me a grandfatherly smile, a twinkle in his eye.

"Okay," I say, and then shake my head. "Wait, what baby?"

"The baby." The doctor gestures to my belly. "You didn't know you were pregnant?"

"EVERYTHING OKAY?" Lincoln's brow creases as he navigates the deep grooves in the mountain road. He took one look at my face when I left the doctor and kept quiet. I handed him the sheet of paper that said I was free and clear of all diseases. I didn't show him the second piece of paper, the one that told me what was coming in thirty-one weeks.

A baby. The nausea, the bone tiredness makes sense. My weird illness isn't an illness, but morning sickness. The exhaustion, normal. There's something growing in me. *A child.*

Fuck.

How did this happen? I mean, I know how it happened. Jack and I were young and in lust and stupid. In time, I might have loved him. Maybe. I haven't had a chance to examine my feelings for him in the wake of the events around his death. HIs life ended a month ago and so did mine. I'm a dead woman walking.

The doctor was kind; even he could tell I was reeling from the news. He asked me if I wanted to talk about options. I almost laughed. A soon-to-be single mom with a temporary prostitution gig? What options did I have?

He started, "It's not too late—"

I held up my hand. "No," I croak. "Not that." There were pills and procedures to fix my problem. I wouldn't fault a woman for using them. But I was a child of a single mom. Twenty-one years ago, I was the burden and inconvenience. She would've been better off without me. "People told my mom to abort me. She didn't listen." I drop my voice to a whisper. "I'll keep my baby too."

"All right," the doc said gently. "Do you want to hear the heartbeat?"

"There's already a heartbeat?" My voice squeaked from far away.

He nodded. And just like that, the course of my life took a sharp detour, right over Niagara Falls.

"Sierra?" Lincoln calls. The truck hits a pothole and knocks me from my *Thinker* pose.

"Yeah," I say shakily. "I'm good."

His lips press together. I don't sound too convincing.

"Everything's okay," I try again. I have to bluff. I can't jeopardize the one good thing I have going. Seven good things, if you don't count Mason. "I just get a little weird when I go to the doctor. And I need to go back in a month. Birth control stuff," I explain further. Lincoln's face remains impassive. "I'll pay for it myself."

"No need. The boys and I voted. We're going to cover it. Perk of the job."

"Okay." They don't want to risk me getting pregnant. *Too late.* A hysterical laugh bubbles up my throat. I strangle it before it escapes.

I'm having a baby.

I'm quiet the rest of the way and Lincoln doesn't push me.

We pull into the yard. Saint and Mason are there, chatting over the grill of a truck. They fall silent as we roll by and give me a blank and hostile stare, respectively.

My hand's on the door handle. I want to climb into bed and never get out, not in thirty-one weeks, not to go to the hospital, not ever. My body feels like it's been beaten.

Lincoln parks and catches my hand before I jump out. "Sierra... you don't have to do anything you don't want to do."

He thinks I'm having second thoughts. He has no idea how fucked I am, literally and figuratively. "I know."

He brings my hand to his mouth and kisses it. So sweet.

I don't tell him I'll do anything and everything as long as I can. I need to earn my money. I'll need all I can get so I and this baby can survive.

Elon's sweeping the dining hall when we walk in.

"Everything okay?" he asks.

I force a smile and give him a thumbs up as I head to my room. Behind my closed door, I pull up my shirt and examine my belly. Still pretty flat. No sign of the life growing there, but the bed creaks as I sit, as if the news add pounds to my small frame.

"Oh, baby," I whisper. "What am I gonna do?"

Leave it to Jack to knock me up and die, abandoning me to face the consequences. *Just like a man,* Lynny would say. Her lack of faith never kept her from scrambling to find one. One scraggly biker after another, each more unsuitable than the last. Until she died and left me to fend for myself. I clung to the first man who came along and ended up like this.

Repeat after me: do not trust men. Not even the giant woodsmen lurking outside my door, wondering if they should knock and make sure I'm all right. I'm going to use them and their money. By the time this baby is born, I'll have carved out a new life for myself.

First I have to make sure I can keep this job. Would they toss a pregnant woman out on the streets? Lincoln wouldn't, but a pat on the back and a drop off at a bus stop with a little money amounts to the same thing.

I have maybe three or four months before the guys will notice. I'm eating more—the guys will think I'm just gaining healthy weight. It's cold enough that they won't question me wearing sweaters or hoodies. I bought a few pairs of thick leggings that will stretch.

Morning sickness—the doc said that might go away when I hit the second trimester. So a few weeks. Luckily, I'm not expected to be 'on' until dinner. I can hide in my room and say I'm not a morning person.

Nights belong to the guys. And I'm going to give them their money's worth. Whatever I make will have to sustain me and a baby until I can find a new place to land. Maybe I can grab a bus south. Reach back out to one of my high school friends, or one of Lynny's. Maybe they'll know someone I can stay with, somewhere the Hell Riders will never look. Maybe Dex will have called off the search by then.

Yeah and maybe Saint will offer to babysit and the twins will knit my kid a onesie. I can't expect things to get better. I'd be better off holding my breath until Mason smiles at me.

I have no fucking idea what I'm gonna do. The future feels far away, looming like a monster, a catastrophe too big to understand, overshadowing my real and very present fear of the Hell Riders. If the MC finds me, I won't need to worry about being a single mom. They'll kill me for what happened to Jack.

Don't think about that. I clutch the bedspread and breathe deeply so I don't puke in fear. *Don't think.*

Rubbing my belly, I sit up. Time to change into my slut outfit and wow my regulars. At least I'll eat good until the season ends, or until the guys discover my secret and throw me out. Whichever comes first.

4

S ierra

I HIT the canteen with a swagger. "All clean, boys!" Jagger whoops and high fives one of the twins.

"You guys were gone a long time," Mason says.

"If you're hoping I have some horrific disease, you're not in luck. The doc just spent extra time examining the horns on my head." I smile sweetly. The twins guffaw. Mason shakes his head and looks away.

"Come here, baby." Jagger pulls me into his lap. I slide my white hands over his tattoo sleeves and grind down on him. "How are we doing this?" His cock lies heavy under his jeans. I let my fingers brush it as I pretend to think about the schedule Lincoln and I decided on. The pecking order. The pecker order. Heh.

"How about I put on a show for you tonight?"

"You up for that?"

"Oh yeah," I purr, leaning forward to whisper in his ear as I spear Mason with my eyes. "I'm all over it."

~

MY MOUTH IS dry as I step into the large room. Chairs scrape as the big guys turn. With the light in my face, I can't see their expressions, but I can imagine each one. The twins' mouths falling open in sync. Jagger hooting—his catcall splits the air. Roy and Tommy are in the kitchen cleaning up, but I bet they pause and peek out to see the show. Lincoln and Saint will control their expressions even as lust fills their eyes. Mason will sneer, but watch me the whole time.

I strut on my makeshift stage, balancing on four-inch heels—the highest I could find. I'm glad I had the forethought to get Lincoln to stop at a larger general store before the doctor's appointment. A white basque hugs my breasts and waist, ending just above the garter belt slung around my hips. The garter straps frame my pussy and almost nonexistent thong, holding up sheer white stockings. I look like a bride on her wedding night, sweet and virginal, dressed in white from hair clip to heels.

The music starts. *Like a Virgin* by Madonna. Jagger has a sense of humor and well-stocked iPod. He promised to let me put together some dance playlists later. Maybe tonight, after I fuck him.

I lick my lips as I sway, tasting lipstick. The only spot of color on me: my red, red lips. Red as the apple that tempted Eve.

Half blind from the spotlight, I dance around the table. Chairs creak as the guys twist to watch. Hands reach for me. Out of the corner of my eye, Mason glowers. I twirl away, an angel, a vision, a wet dream. The rooms grows hot, scented with sweat and sawdust.

The song changes. *Born to Fuck,* my hips chant, and they don't lie. I sidle up to Saint and take his hand, balancing as I use his chair to step onto the table. I crawl toward Lincoln sitting at the head. Hands run over my body, help me to my feet. I twerk and mouth the words to Benassi's *Satisfaction.* Hands drift up my legs and I guide them to slip my thong down my legs. I clamber down and give lap dances to whoever's willing. Roy and Tommy wave me on, and Mason refuses to uncross his arms. I spend extra time waving my ass in his face, just to get a reaction.

The set ends with me straddling Jagger.

"Your room?" I whisper and he lifts me without hesitation. We hit the door to his room and collapse, giggling, onto the bed.

"Sierra, alone at a last."

I roll my eyes, but I'm cool with Jagger, his outrageous statements and clichéd jokes. He's the perfect choice for tonight's lay. For one thing, he's too busy showing off to look at me closely, to peer under my plastic smile. I'm acting hard tonight, with an ingénue outfit and femme fatale lipstick, and Jagger is the perfect audience.

He grabs his iPod and puts on *Closer* by Nine Inch Nails. "Come 'ere."

I whore-crawl across the bed and kneel between his legs, my fingers busy with his jeans zipper.

"You're hot as fuck," he tells me as I grip his cock and play with it, wrapping my hand around it and stroking it. He moans and sinks back against the pillows lining the headboard. I grab a condom and sheath him quickly so I can pop him into my mouth. I bob my head in time to the music. Breath hisses between Jagger's teeth and his lower half tenses. When his eyes close, I smirk to myself. Tonight's gonna be easy. Good thing, too, because I'm wrung out like a used sponge, my chest tight with unshed tears. Maybe Jagger will cum and fall right to sleep so I can cry my eyes out in the shower.

I hollow my cheeks, sucking like my life depends on drinking Jagger's sperm. He clutches the sheets and groans, his body tense like he's being crucified.

A new song comes on—Marilyn Manson's cover of *Personal Jesus*. I bob my head double time.

"Whoa, whoa." Jagger grabs my shoulders. "Not so fast."

I slow but he lifts me off, pulling me to him. I let him maneuver me into switching spots with him. On his knees before me, he whips off his shirt and tosses it. The ladder of his abs stretch and flex, dazzling me. The side of his mouth hitches up as he comes close again, blond locks falling around his stubbled, narrow face. His eyelashes are blond and long as a girl's. I blink away my stupor as he settles between my legs.

"Wh-what are you doing?" I ask.

Jagger's busy fiddling with the straps on my garters. "You're clean, right? I'm gonna taste you."

"This... this..."

"Shhh." He squeezes my ass. "Just relax."

"Okay, sure. Fine." I close my eyes and my problems loom. I'm broke, I'm homeless, my boyfriend is dead and I'm on the run, I'm soon to be a single mom. *Yeah okay, Jagger, I'll just relax.*

Jagger's tongue hits a spot with a deep inner itch.

He breathes into my pussy and I jerk back so hard my head hits the headboard. Fuck. Jagger's new nickname is 'Giraffe' because, man, he has an amazing tongue.

"What about you?" I pant, and push up to straddle his

face. I sixty-nine him, fighting my way to get his dick in my mouth. He thrust shallowly, moaning into my pussy. His fingers dig into my hip, soldering to my skin, holding me still as he laps at me.

"Oooh, Jagger." I take my mouth off him long enough to make meaningless sounds. His tongue does unspeakable things and suddenly I'm speaking a made up language.

"Shhhh." He nuzzles me. I babble some more.

His dirty blond head dips, his tongue stroking along a needy part of me. It's my turn to hiss and grip the sheet. His tongue feels bigger, digging deep, swiping the side of my inner wall, turning the swirling sensation there into a maelstrom threatening to wreck me.

"Jagger, I... fuck." I twist in his grip. He pins me down and keeps lapping. A deep moan vibrates against my pussy; he's enjoying this as much as I am. Maybe more.

He's the client. I remind myself. *Lie back and think of baseball. No, not that, don't delay your orgasm. That'd be rude. Think of Mason—imagine him—no, not Mason, not him.*

My limbs writhe, straining for something just out of reach. Jagger's tongue flicks my clit and my legs start shaking. I can't think of anything. The long thin string of pleasure vibrates faster, spreading through me entirely. It snaps. I convulse hard, my legs snapping around Jagger's head so hard I almost take it off. He laughs straight into my opening. *Fuck.* I force myself to go loose and flop to my side.

He rises up wiping his chin, pushes apart my knees, and enters me.

My muscles clench around him, tightening and releasing as waves of my climax roll through me. He plants his tanned arm by my head, pulls my leg over his shoulder and slaps his hips into mine. I grit my teeth and hang on, riding through the end of my orgasm and straight into another.

Jagger pulls out, flips me onto hands and knees and pounds me from behind. I squawk, arms flailing. I overbalance and fall to my face. Still Jagger keeps pounding. My entire lower half is sensitive. My toes curl, my backside and backs of my thighs grow warm from him slamming into me. Another climax catches me by surprise and I shatter.

"Fuck, Sierra, fuck," Jagger gasps. He roots deep within me with a final groan. I glance around the messy room, marveling that the building is still standing. Each orgasm shook my world apart.

Jagger's sigh echoes through me.

"That was..." My tongue feels too large for my mouth. "Amazing."

"I took a pill," Jagger mumbles, drooling onto the pillow, halfway passed out.

"Fuck," I tell him, and he laughs like Lincoln did the first time he and I fucked: with surprise and delight.

I WAKE to the sound of pouring rain, a waterfall rushing past the window.

I raise my head. I must have passed out like a dude. Not surprising, given the day I had.

Jagger is asleep next to me, his tanned limbs loose on the bed. In the shadows his face is flawless, framed with angelic locks. He looks sweet and cuddle-worthy, but I can't wait to get out of bed. I'm not here to cuddle. I'm here to fuck. As I leave the room, I think, *one down, seven to go.*

The living area is dark. I hover in the hall and listen for signs of life, but it's late and these men worked a full day.

They'll all be asleep. I need to wash the cum and sweat and memory away and crawl into bed, alone. Lincoln would welcome me again, but I can't, not tonight. Not with all these secrets beating in my chest.

Something makes me detour past the table where I perform nightly, past the kitchen and out the door. Beyond the building overhang, mud puddles grow to lakes. Beyond the yard, the forest shivers with rain. I stand between the building and sheet of water falling over the eaves, and suck in clean lungfuls of air.

I don't know what the future holds. I do know if I survive this, finish the gig and have the baby, I'm never having sex again. I'm swearing off men forever. Lynny was right—they're trouble. Unlike Lynny, I'm not gonna hold out hope I'll find a good one. My mom wasted too many years going from guy to guy, looking for the one who would save us. Support us, treat her right. It never happened. She died thirteen months ago, and I followed in her failed footsteps—ran to Jack, thinking he'd take care of me.

Now I'm in the lumberjacks' barracks, surrounded by men. I've got a few months to earn some money and hide from the Hell Riders until I can escape them forever. But after this: no more. I'm never trusting or touching a guy again. I'll break the cycle before my baby is born.

A bright fleck breaks the darkness, glows in the corner of my eye. A burning eye—the end of a cigarette. As I startle back against the building, Mason emerges from the shadows. He sees me and stops in his tracks. For a second he looks uncertain.

I turn away from him and wipe my eyes, rearranging my hair. He might think my face got wet from the rain. Or not. I don't really care.

He starts forward and I hold up a hand. I don't want pity from him.

He offers the cigarette. I shake my head and turn away, walking to the opposite edge of the building. I feel his eyes on me as he takes his time finishing his smoke. Eventually he heads inside, leaving me alone, outside, in the rain.

"So how are we doing this?" I ask Elon and Oren. They stand between me and the door, redheaded monoliths with similar excited, but uncertain expressions. A few minutes ago, I was dancing on a table for everyone. I grabbed one of the twin's hands and pulled him toward his room. I didn't know the other would follow. "This is your room, right?" The space is neat but haphazard, with furniture awkwardly placed around two twin beds pushed together in the center of the room. "Is this your bed?"

"We share a bed," they say at the same time.

"You... okay." I feel like a tiny woodland creature scurrying at the feet of two red oaks, so I stop looking up at them. Tonight's strip tease starred a black bra and thong under one of Lincoln's work shirts. From the wood rising under the dining table, my LumberJane outfit was a hit. I lost the shirt and bra during my act, but not the thong. I hook my fingers into the straps now, ready to draw it down.

"No, let me do that." One of the twins goes to one knee in front of me. I suck in a breath as he pinches the fabric between large thumbs and forefingers, and peels the scrap of cloth away. The powerful man performing such a delicate movement opens my own personal floodgates, and when he raises his head to fix his blue eyes on mine, I can't speak.

"Sierra? What do you want us to do?"

I know exactly what I want, though I can barely find my voice. "Strip."

The two mirror images get busy obeying, unbuttoning jeans, peeling back sleeves to show tautly muscled forearms, drawing off undershirts while the shadows ripple over the insane perfection of their abs and chests. My mouth goes dry as all available moisture pools down below.

Finally, they stand naked before me, a mirror image of ragged red beards and excited blue eyes. Their hands hovering awkwardly in the air. Oren's dick tilts to the left, Elon's to the right.

I giggle like Jagger.

"Okay. All right. Condoms." As the guys fumble with protection, I back up until my thighs hit the bed, and sit down, careful of the crack in the center of this makeshift king. I point at random.

"You get me first while he watches. Then we switch."

Then you jack off facing each other and I'll watch, I add silently. Might as well cross all the things off my bucket list before I swear off sex forever.

The guys nod and I sink to my knees before them. "But first," I whisper, and close my hands around their cocks. One jerks slightly as my fingers touch it, a reaction repeated in the second, on delay. *A dick in the hand is worth two in the bush. Or something.*

I dart my head to the left, then to the right, sucking lightly on the two heads as their owners suck in their breaths overhead. *Two heads are better than one.* I snicker and the left tilted dick jumps, pulsing a little. Oren takes a step back.

Sierra, slow down.

"Get on the bed. Here." I leap up and push the two beds apart so the guys can sit facing each other. I direct them into place and kneel again, keeping them within hand's reach while I suck one and then the other. "Relax," I say as Elon's thighs tighten. Their legs and chests are dusted with red hair and freckles. "Do you like that?" I loll his cock around in my mouth. His mouth falls open but he can't answer. Their balls draw up tight. This isn't going to last long.

I snap up, straddle Oren's lap backwards, and drive down. At the same time, I guide Elon's flagpole into my mouth. The instant their dicks enter the hot, wet parts of me, they erupt. I hum around Elon's cock, reveling in his choked curses and wild thrashing on the bed. Oren sags over me, mumbling into my hair. I sit up slowly, lick my lips and smile. "Again?"

THREE NIGHTS IN, and my life falls into a rhythm, an easy back and forth to a soundtrack of men's voices and heavy machinery. I sleep all day and emerge for dinner, laughing and talking and entertaining the guys until it's time for them to clear the table for my dance.

Jagger and I make elaborate playlists with everything Nicki Minaj to 80s power ballads. I figure out the guy's preferred music styles, and on their night, I dance to their favorite songs. Or I chose songs that make me think of them. *Booty Shorts* by Gucci Mane and *Lady Marmalade* for Saint. *The Man* by the Killers, *Girl Money* by the Kix and *Yankin* by Lady for Lincoln.

Elon and Oren: *Identical Twins* by Crumbächer and *Who Can It Be Now?* by Men at Work.

Attention by Charlie Puth for Jagger. *You Can't Always Get What You Want* by the Rolling Stones. And, of course, *Moves*

Like Jagger by Maroon 5. He got up and danced with me during the last one.

Lincoln was right about Roy and Tommy—they both are perfectly polite, but decline a night with me and wave away any lap dances. Two less guys to fuck and I'm so grateful, I dedicate a performance to them and go with a food theme: *Cherry Pie* by Warrant, *Cookie* by R. Kelly Cookie and *Pour Some Sugar on Me* by Def Leppard.

But for Mason... ah, Mason. I find a song by Cruel Youth called *Hate Fuck* for him. And *Undisclosed Desires* by Muse. Although the last song might have more to do with how I feel about him. His gaze cuts me so hard during the set I have to force myself not to retreat behind Lincoln or Jagger. Even Saint's carefully blank mask would be easier to face than Mason's smoldering hatred.

"Well, Mason?" I ask when the last chord fades. Roy and Tommy have already disappeared, along with the twins. I'll bet Elon and Oren went to jack off and pass out on their Franken-bed. Last night I danced and stroked and did everything I could to get them upright so I could fuck them a second, then a third time. Gotta love their youthful stamina. We fucked so much I have rug burn on my boobs and back from their rusty chest hair.

Mason stares carefully at the wall.

"Mason," I singsong. He can't ignore me forever. We are not twelve. "It's your night. I don't usually sleep with guys prettier than me, but it's part of the gig—"

"No."

"C'mon man, it's been awhile. You obviously need a good lay." Jagger spasms with laughter.

"Shut the fuck up," Mason mutters in his work mate's direction. "I don't need pity pussy."

"Then I suggest Prozac," I say sweetly. Mason knifes up,

ready with some insult, but before he can stab me, Lincoln stands up between us.

"Come on, Sierra."

I let the crew chief pull me into his room. After he shuts the door, I breathe easy. The tightness in my chest from the day I learned I was pregnant hasn't gone away.

"How you doin'?" Lincoln asks. He stands between me and the door, a solid obstacle to anyone or anything that would come to get me. *Safe,* his broad body whispers to mine in the dim light. His dark eyes invite me to break.

"How do you think I'm doing?" I ask.

His sigh washes through me, settling into my bones as I melt onto the bed. "I hoped Mason would come around."

I shrug. "I didn't do anything to him."

"I know. Give him time."

I gnaw my lip. Should I keep offering to fuck him? "I don't want to be annoying. Like a little sister."

"Trust me, Sierra," Lincoln stretches out next to me on the bed, and my whole body starts to tingle. "No one here thinks of you as a sister."

5

Sierra

MORNINGS in the lodge are my favorite. The lodge empties out just after breakfast, long before the scent of coffee entices me from my bed. *What to Expect When You're Expecting* advises against coffee, but I've already given up wine, and I don't want to lose my will to live. I'm careful to drink only a little of the tarlike stuff, adding tons of milk and sugar. Baby doesn't appreciate caffeine on an empty stomach.

I stroke my belly, studying myself in the mirror. The smallest curve, the slightest convex arc. Not enough for a man to notice, unless he was searching for it. Nothing a sweatshirt can't hide. By the time fall is here, I'll be swimming in sweaters. The guys will think all of Saint's good food finally took hold. I suck in a breath, hold my stomach in, like a teenager worried she's getting fat.

Such a trivial worry, compared to the terror my life holds now.

I'm halfway to the kitchen, stomach gurgling after all the contorting I did in front of the mirror. If I keep raiding the fridge every few hours, I will become fat.

The sound of motorcycle pipes has me freeze.

Oh no, not here. Not when I've come so far, and tried so hard to hide.

Shouts in the yard—whoever is here was expected. I scuttle into the kitchen just as the door opens and Saint walks in, holding a helmet and wearing the largest leather jacket ever made. He stops when he sees me. His boots are spattered with mud.

"Sierra?"

I find my voice. "You ride?" I try for a smile, but it slips from my face.

He cocks his head, studying me. We've come to a truce, Saint and I. He feeds me, I eat his food and he doesn't send Lincoln to get a different woman.

"On my day off. Got a bike in the back. Took it out to make sure it's still running."

"Ah." I don't ask him why he's off when everyone else is working. As far as I can tell, he announces what he wants to do, and everyone tiptoes around making it work.

I realize I'm staring and drop my gaze to the floor. "So," I say shakily. "We should talk about... your night."

His expression goes blank, the way it did when he first saw me, or when I dance. He brushes by me, putting his helmet on the kitchen counter.

"Lincoln told me I should talk to you about it. First."

A pause. He opens the fridge door, peers inside. "Have you eaten?"

"I had a biscuit earlier." Saliva pools in my mouth. Now

that I'm getting six meals a day, the nausea has retreated. But I'm always up for more food. "I could eat."

"What are you in the mood for?" He solemnly regards the contents of the fridge. Food is serious business to Saint.

"Is there any chocolate?" I blurt, and wish I could take it back.

"You got a craving, girl?" His head is hidden in the fridge, but I hear the smile.

"No! Not that. Not a craving." Only pregnant women get cravings, right? Saint twists toward me, and I search his face for any sign that he knows my condition. Why else would he use the word 'craving?' "I just love chocolate. I used to eat if for breakfast. Sometimes I wouldn't eat anything but chocolate all day."

His eyes narrow.

"But I'm good. I can wait for lunch. I'm not... I don't have a craving." My hands are hovering around my belly. Saint fixes his gaze on them and I force them to drop to my hips. Gah, it's like he can read my mind. *Think non-pregnant thoughts.*

"Come on." He heads down the hall, motioning me to follow. I feel like Jack in the Beanstalk, tiptoeing behind the giant.

Saint's room is the very last, and bigger than anyone else's. As I enter he's turning, a large chocolate bar in his hand. I could cry with happiness, but then I spot the shelves behind him.

"Holy crap," I shout. Saint's room is filled with just about the only thing that can distract me from chocolate.

Books.

"You read?" he rumbles after I've spun in a circle, taking in the rows and rows and stacks and stacks. There's enough to fill a library and then some.

"Uh, yeah," I scoff, until I realize he's kidding me. "Do you? Have you read all these?"

"Yep."

"Awesome," I breathe, turning to the nearest shelf and running a reverent hand down the spines. There's everything from math textbooks to big printed bestsellers. A faded copy of *Call of the Wild*, right next to the bed.

"You like to read?"

"Yes." I blink, near tears. Saint's room smells like chocolate and a library. My favorite smells. Wherever I was, wherever my mother dragged me in her crazy hippie wanderlust or loyalty to a random biker man, I'd settle with books and chocolate and I'd know I was home.

I kept tracing titles with my fingers. Saint had a varied collection. Classics, mysteries, even romance and business psychology. Some covers are faded, others have creased spines and dirty edges. When I come to one showing a woman hugging her big pregnant belly, I stop breathing for a second. "These books—can I borrow some? I'll bring them back."

"Take what you like."

I step away and pretend to peruse other titles, grabbing a few at random before returning to slip the pregnancy guide into a pile. I don't know what an eight-foot 300 pound guy is doing with a book like *What to Expect When You're Expecting*, but I'm not about to ask him why.

Actually, I do know. The sight of Saint is enough to make a girl pregnant.

Yesterday I saw him in the shower, eyes closed, water streaming over his obsidian skin, running in sleek rivulets over the planes of his chest and over his pebbled abs. He turned slightly, and a dark, snaking monster poked out from a granite-carved thigh. I scurried out before he caught me, rushed to my room and got myself off in a few soft touches. After that glimpse through the half-cracked door, I would've been pregnant, if I wasn't already.

Maybe that's why he has the book.

Once the pregnancy manual is safely hidden between a few romance novels and a thick thriller, I turn, clutching the books close. Saint has his back to me, rifling through a few piles before turning.

"Here." He thrusts a book at me. "Read this."

"*Sex at Dawn*?" I turn the title into a question mark. "Is it a romance novel?"

"Non-fiction."

I frown and turn it over to read the back description. Saint motions me to sit, so I do, setting down my other finds, opening the book.

I look up fifteen minutes later, blinking. "Humans were meant to be poly."

Saint's sitting a few feet away, on a trunk of some sort. His lips split over white teeth when he grins. "You read fast."

"I used to read through my classes." Lynny moved us around a lot, I was always behind. I learned to read through text books to catch up. As a result, I never was held back a grade. I would've graduated, if not at the top of my class, then at least not anywhere near the bottom. But then Lynny died, and I didn't go back to school. I was too busy following her questionable example, hanging around a motorcycle club and attaching myself to the nearest available guy who looked like he wouldn't slap me around. And look where that got me.

"Here." Saint hands me the candy bar. "Eat that. You look like you're about to pass out."

"Thanks," I mutter. I hoover down the chewy chocolate and relax, one hand on the pile of books as if they give me strength. Saint says nothing, his expression signals nothing, and he sits with his arms crossed over his great chest, chocolate eyes firmly fixed on me. When I'm done eating, he motions to the trash can where I can throw the wrapper, but makes no move to say anything more or kick me out.

The sugar gives me courage to meet his stare. "Tonight... do you want to fuck me?"

He scratches his stubbled chin, still watching me. He doesn't move, but I feel pieced apart, each portion of my body separated and weighed against some unseen balance. Perhaps he's wondering if I'm strong enough to take him. I flush just thinking about it, remembering his naked body in the shower. My pussy tingles at the look in his eye. "Not tonight," he says finally. "Saturday. Rest all day, then come to me."

I STAND IN THE SHOWER, letting the hot water soothe my hurts away. The tightness in my chest has eased somewhat, after the visit with Saint and the loan of some books. I already started reading the pregnancy one. It's pretty generic, bland in some parts, a little scary in others. There are so many variables. So many things that could go wrong. But just to get a child, so many things have to go right. Maybe things will work out.

I'm about to finish up when footsteps echo around me. I'm alone in the big communal shower. Saint went out for an errand in the truck, and the rest of the guys are still working. As far as I know, the lodge and entire lot is empty.

"Saint?" I call, my voice quavering in the empty space. The footsteps pause. Before I can turn the water off and grab a towel, Mason walks in, barefoot, shirtless, wearing jeans. "Mason? What are you doing here?"

He doesn't answer. His gaze sweeps over my naked form and his lips twist.

I reach for the water knob.

"No," his angry voice rings out. I stand small and naked and vulnerable under the warm spray, as he paces forward and stops when the water spatters the hem of his jeans. His breath rasps in and out, his tanned skin flushed at the tips of his cheekbones. Hate in his dark eyes. All his unexplained rage, directed at me.

He takes another step forward, the movement drawing my eyes down, and I see his arousal, even through the thick fabric of his jeans. I open my mouth to say something when he gives me another harsh order.

"Face the wall."

Numb, I do as he says.

"Hands on the tile."

I plant my palms, more to hold myself up than to obey. My legs are parted just a little.

The sound of the water changes, drumming against a man's hard back and chest and solid jeans. I wonder if the water running over his face does anything to soften his expression, the anger he holds like armor between us. Then his hand clamps down on the back of my neck, holding me rigid, pressing my forehead against the wall. My body goes weak as his fingers tighten alongside my throat. For a moment, everything goes dark, just the sound of water slapping our bodies, Mason's breath hissing by my ear.

"Fucking whore," he mutters.

I lick my lips and work my mouth up and down before I'm brave enough to answer. "Whore, cocksucker, slut—you really need to work on your insults."

"Shut up." His grip changes, his hand sliding under my chin, holding me upright. His thumb strokes my pulse. His other arm jerks in the corner of my vision. My fists tighten on the slick wall as Mason's breathing grows rapid. He's beating off, I'm sure of it. His cock aimed at my backside. I make a little noise and his finger's tighten on my throat. I'll have bruises tonight. I'll have to cover them with makeup, or explain them to Lincoln.

"Anita," he groans, and I stiffen. What the fuck?

"Mason," I start, and his fingers tighten, biting and cruel. "No," I wriggle. My skin is wet, it makes it easy to slip out of his grasp. Or perhaps once I actually fight him he lets me go.

I turn and meet his glare. I was right, his jeans are open just enough for him to hold his cock. Rivulets run down the tight V leading to his crotch.

What the fuck do you think you're doing? His eyes say, narrowed under angry brows. The hand on my arm tries to turn me back to face the wall.

"No," I say. "You look at me when you fuck me."

He tilts his head and water runs down that angelic face, twisted into a demon's. Will he ever look at me with anything but disgust?

I stand my ground, as authoritative as I can be without clothes on. The water's turning cool.

Fine, then. He tugs my arm, pulling me down. "Kneel."

I obey, lowering carefully. His left hand takes a hold on my wet hair as he guides his cock toward my lips.

"Suck."

Pussy tingling, I take a deep breath and open my mouth.

Water pours over both of us, blurring my vision. He's warm in my mouth and I hum a little, angling my head, adjusting. I reach up to help and he shakes his head. *No hands.* Meanwhile, his hands move my head this way and that, controlling me. I let myself go limp and embrace his unspoken commands. His hand moving my head up and down in a rough rhythm. *Like this.* The beat of his hips, driving his cock further into my mouth. *Don't stop.* A pinch as his grip tightens in my hair. *That's it. Take it all.*

I choke, hands suspended in the air above his hard thighs. My tears mingle with the shower spray. He tugs me off, his grip sharp enough to bring tears to my eyes. A breath, and he forces me back down. I let my spine loosen, my whole body a puppet in the hands of a master. A groan tells me it'll be over soon. Something salty flows over my tongue and then Mason pulls back. I twitch my face away, eyes closed as the shower washes everything away.

A gentle touch on my jaw. *Good girl.* I reach up to cover his hand, but he's already stepping away, turning off the water and walking off in wet jeans. I'm still on my knees, wondering what the fuck just happened.

LATER THAT NIGHT, I lay in bed stroking my belly, *What to Expect When You're Expecting* beside me, hidden under a large print thriller.

"You doin' okay?" Jagger slouches in the doorframe, waiting until I wave him in.

"Yeah. Just tired."

"We wear you out?" His eyes crinkle with humor.

I laugh. "You know it."

"Seriously, though," he sits by my feet, picking them up and plopping them in his lap. Still not big on boundaries is Jagger. "You holding up okay?"

"Oh yeah," I yawn and stretch. His thumb strokes up the arch of my foot, and I melt into a moan. "Oh, do that again."

"Everyone treating you right?"

"You sound like Lincoln." The big crew chief came in after tonight's dance to quiz me carefully on what I thought of the job thus far.

"What did he say?"

"He just wanted to know if I was cool with everything. I told him so far there weren't any OSHA violations."

Jagger keeps kneading my feet, chuckling. "Who's night is it?"

"Uhhh, I think it's still Mason's." *Except Mason and I already had our moment. Sorta.* "I don't know. Saint wants me Saturday. I did everyone else, except Roy and Tommy."

"Mmmhhmmm," Jagger murmurs knowingly.

"What? What do you know?"

"It's Roy and Tommy."

"Yeah, and... They're so sweet. I think they like watching but they always go off alone afterwards."

"You mean they always go off together." He emphasizes the word 'together.'

My mouth drops open. "What? No..."

"Yes." Jagger waggles his eyebrows. "Shhh. Don't ask don't tell. But we're cool with it." His voice lowers. "The other crews might not be. But Lincoln made it clear he was and we keep our shit tight. He's such a good leader, perfect safety record, the company will give him anything he wants."

"Just to be clear: Roy and Tommy are together," I spell out. Jagger nods. Gay lumberjacks. Who knew? "No wonder they don't want a night."

"So that frees up your schedule."

I shrug. If Jagger is angling for an extra night, he's going to have to do all the work. Although, if he rubs my feet like this on my nights off, I might jump him anyway.

Jagger laughs and I realize I said my last thought out loud. "So sleeping with all these guys? You really don't mind?"

I shrug again. "I'm cool with it. Saint gave me this book." I sift through my pile of borrows, careful to keep the pregnancy guide hidden. "It theorizes how human communities used to be poly. Polyamorous," I clarify when Jagger's eyebrows go up. "Specifically, one woman would mate with multiple males."

Jagger's hands still as he stares at me.

"What? I didn't make this up!" I page through the book. "They think they have evidence based on physical qualities. For example, the penis is shaped like a shovel so it can scoop semen out of the vagina before making its own deposit. And women cry out during orgasm—which could've been a way of calling more men to come inseminate her."

Jagger's eyes are frozen on my face. I wave my hands in the air as if they can help me explain.

"They think it explains a lot about why women take longer to orgasm. And premature ejaculation. If their theories are correct, a guy finishing early would be a trait that meant their seed was the first in, and the first to take root. Evolution would select for it. I don't know," I finish, mumbling and not meeting Jagger's wide eyes. "I think it make sense."

"Sierra, I..." Jagger keeps shaking his head. My foot is still between his hands, and I attempt to remove it. He hangs on and keeps massaging it, even as he looks at me like I'm a zoo animal. "I don't know what to say. This is not what I expected to talk about."

"It's interesting to think about, anyway."

"Yes, it definitely is. But what about your feelings? Forget premature ejaculation and natural selection. How are you feeling, being with a bunch of guys?"

I open my mouth to answer, and a shadow falls across the door. Mason steps in my room, rapping his fist on my door as if he didn't just barge into my space, knocking as an afterthought. "Am I interrupting?"

Mouth still open, I try to think of what to say. Jagger frowns. "What are you doing here?"

"It's my night, right?" The beautiful man is already turning away. "Come to my room in fifteen."

"Uh, wha..." I manage to get out before Jagger's on his feet.

"It was your night. Last night. You passed. She's resting."

Now my mouth is hanging open at Jagger defending me like this. His shoulders bunch up, hands curling to fists. Mason pivots neatly and the two guys face off. They're not as huge as the rest of the crew, but they've got enough anger and muscles to cause some danger.

"Hey, wait," I say weakly. "It's okay." I look at Mason, wondering if he enjoyed himself in the shower so much that he wanted more. I don't want to mention it; it seemed weird that Mason was at the lodge while everyone was on shift. I don't want to get him in trouble.

Me defending Mason is also weird.

"I'm all right," I tell Jagger. "Mason's right. It's his turn. I'll be right there." I stand up and busy myself organizing my books. What should I wear?

When I turn back, Mason is gone. Jagger has his arms folded across his chest. "You don't have to do this."

"It's fine." Despite everything, I'm excited, a telltale tingle creeping up my thighs. "He's just grumpy. It's probably all an act for attention."

"No, it isn't. He's dangerous." Jagger leans on the door, chewing his lip.

I shrug, even as excitement ripples through my body, remembering the water running over Mason's impossible cheekbones, his harsh commands. *No*, I tell myself severely, *it was not hot. It was rude. You did not like it.*

But I did.

A few minutes later, I wander down to Mason's room. My nemesis stands at the door, jaw clenched. He turns and walks in, expecting me to follow. His room is neat, no books or clutter or signs of personality. The bed looks like no one has ever slept on it. *Maybe he sleeps upside down, hanging from the ceiling, like a bat.* A giggle escapes before I can stop it.

Mason's black brows knit together. "Face the wall," he orders.

"This again?" I mutter, but turn toward the wooden dresser as he comes at me. His hand claps against my bottom, making me jump. The spank doesn't hurt, but I look back at him, curious.

"Stay where you are." His arms reach around me and he roughly undoes my jeans and peels them down. I hang onto the dresser for balance.

"Are you going to frisk me?" I can't keep from snarking. *Shut up, Sierra.* I tell myself a second before he says the same.

"No underwear?" he asks, and I shrug. I changed from my pajama bottoms into jeans for the walk down the hall, but left my camisole. No bra or underwear; I didn't see the point. "Fucking slut."

"That's me," I murmur and suck in a breath as he shoves his fingers into my pussy. Not because it hurt—because it felt good.

I twist to see his reaction. If he expected to dry fuck me, he's outta luck. His eyes widen as his fingers glide right in.

"That's right," I whisper as every cell in my body focuses around the welcome intruder. "I'm fucking wet for you. Must be your pretty, pretty face."

His eyes are hostile, his fingers stretching and reaching, thrusting crudely. He looks like he wants to hurt me, but he can't. I'm too wet.

I laugh right in his face. "Is it hard, Mason? Being the prettiest one in camp?"

"Shut the fuck up," he breathes, his pupils growing until his irises are thin umber rings. "I'm gonna fuck you so hard. You're gonna do what I say, because I'm paying. You're the whore."

"Your wish is my command." I twist off his fingers and slide to the floor, slowly, so I can watch his body clench and eyes catch fire. Halfway down he grips my hair, hard enough to sting, and presents his wet fingers to my lips.

"Suck it, whore," he orders. "Show me what you can do."

I yank down his boxers and engulf his cock instead. He hisses, staggering back until his calves hit the bed I cup his balls and hum as I work my tongue around his length, dragging it along the bottom and poking it into the dent under the flared head. He grips my hair harder, but I press forward, ignoring the pain in my scalp, taking him deep.

"Fuck."

"Your wish is my command." I rise and peel off my shirt in one movement. My small breasts bounce, catching his eye. I use the distraction to make my move, pressing my pale body against him, embracing him like a lover.

He turns us and rolls so I'm on my back. His hands lock around my wrists and wrench them away from him.

"Don't touch me," he grits out.

"Hard to fuck without touching you," I shoot back, and he frees a hand to swat between my legs. His palm connects with my pussy and I yelp. "Fuck." I buck against the bed, fighting to get my wrists free from the punishing shackle of his right hand. Evil glints in his eyes as he smacks me again, this time hitting my right haunch like a rider encouraging a horse.

"I make the rules," he warns and I nod. Fine. My pussy is too eager for me to keep arguing.

Smirking as if he knows how hot his dominance makes me, he rolls a condom on his glistening length.

"I'm clean," I say automatically and he gives me a look that makes my cheeks burn. He wants to fuck a dirty, dirty whore? Fine. I can play that game.

"Roll over," he commands. "All fours."

"What's the matter, don't want to look me in the face while you fuck? You gonna pretend I'm a little boy?" I taunt. His face darkens and I know I've pushed him too far.

"On your back then," he snaps. "Not like that. Spread your legs. Wider."

As soon as I—bravely—take the vulnerable position, he's on me. He thrusts inside with brutal force, so rough he'd tear me if I wasn't so sopping wet.

"Yes," I can't stop myself from sighing. If I was smart, I'd shut up. Mason slams forward, sending me sliding further onto the bed. Tears pop into my eyes—tears of pleasure.

"Come on," I grunt, locking my ankles behind his iron hard back. "Prove you're more than just a pretty face."

His hips snap forward and he drives into me, so deep stars fill my vision. My nails dig into his smooth skin. I could claw his sleek shoulders, leave red marks marring his perfect tan. I scratch down his back and grip his tight ass to pull him deeper. His glare stabs me, penetrating me in a different way.

I close my eyes.

"No," he barks. "Look at me when I fuck you."

"That's my line," I laugh. His expression says murder, but his dick sings a sweet, rhythmic song. I plant my heels on the bed and thrust up, mashing my pelvis against his in time to the deep, sexual beat. For as long as I live, I will remember the rocking strength of his body, the perfect bow of his lips tempting, daring me to risk it all for a kiss. My orgasm gathers in the far corners of my body, rivulets of pleasure running through me, head to groin to feet. It slams into me, breaking me, wringing me out, leaving me breathless.

I will forever compare this fuck to all others. I will have sex dreams about this glorious hate fuck. The best sex of my life.

"Here." He tosses something at me. Money. The bills smack me in the face.

Shaking, weak with anger and melting pleasure, I rise and slip on my clothes, my tip crushed in my fist.

"Not bad for a whore," he yawns.

"I'm not a whore." I give him a hard smile, as friendly as a kick to the gut. "Whores fuck for money. I'm here for the sex." I toss the bills on the bed, and swagger from his room.

IN THE MIDDLE of the night, demons rise in my mind.

"Sierra's a hot little piece."

"Yep," Jack agrees, taking a pull on his beer.

"She's been around the club, what, a year?"

"Little longer. Her mother used to hang around the Hell Pit before she died."

"That's right. Wannabe old lady. Hit by a car and left her girl all alone," Dex says thoughtfully. "Dried up old hag, the mother. But the daughter... she grew up just right."

"Yeah," Jack answers. Through the screen door, I watch my boyfriend bob his head, eager to agree with the club leader, so oblivious to the satanic glint in Dex's eye. "Sierra's great."

"Mmm." Dex takes a hit of his joint, passes it to Jack. The light from the silent TV reflects off his brass rings. "You know how it is in the club. Before you take an old lady, you gotta give her to me."

I suck in a breath, jerking back in the shadows where I've been hiding. I knew Dex was up to something. The president of the whole MC doesn't single out a lowly patch to hang out with, like a school girl desperate for a BFF. Jack was so excited about this meeting, so hopeful. Like the rest of the club, he hero worships Dex. And now we're stuck at Dex's house.

I glance back at the fire pit, where my backpack still sits. I don't want Jack to share me with his club prez. The thought of Dex touching me makes me sick. Should I run? Maybe just walk down the street for a bit, come back when the guys are high and half asleep and no longer in the mood. I can leave my backpack and just say I needed some fresh air. My stomach's not feeling right anyway.

I'm so busy planning my escape I miss Jack mumbling something.

Dex doesn't answer right away. He plucks the joint from Jack's hands and stabs it out. "I think you've waited long enough. Call her inside, Jack. It's time to share."

I jerk awake. For a moment, I'm not alone. Memories lurk in the shadows. Jack coming out the door to call my name. Me hiding alongside the house, holding my breath until he goes back inside, tells Dex I must've run. The slam of the front door followed by the roar of pipes: the prez leaving.

Is that what really happened? Must be: when I went back inside to Jack, Dex was gone.

The next thing I remember is the sound of the gun. The shot echoes in my memory as I scrub my face. Try as I might, I don't remember what happened before the gun. Before the blood.

I remember what happened after all too well.

I stare at the ceiling, willing it to turn grey with the dawn. I can't sleep, I can't settle. I've spent too much time on the run, paying penance for that night, Jack's death.

But here in the lodge, with a chance to breathe, maybe I can remember why Jack had to die.

6

E ^{lon}

"HEY, REDHEAD."

I stop in the hall even though I don't want to. Jagger sits splayed on his bed, a cloud of smoke over his head.

"No smoking in the lodge," I parrot. "You know Lincoln doesn't like it."

Jagger rolls his eyes, but he rises to lean against the window and blow smoke out the crack. I wait while he stubs the joint out and turns to me with an obnoxious smile, hands splayed to show me the obvious. Like I'll believe he's done for the night. As soon as I continue to my room, the joint will be back in his mouth.

"What do you want?"

"Can't I say hello to my favorite redhead?"

"What's my name, Jagger?" I wait while he squints at me, lips parting as if he's going to guess.

"Okay." Jagger laughs like he told a hilarious joke. "You got me. I never can tell the difference between you two."

"I'm Elon," I say patiently.

"Right. You got any booze left, Elon?"

I shrug. I have a bottle of port I'm saving for the first day of fall. My tradition. But Lincoln doesn't like us drinking on season. One of his funny rules.

Not that it stops Jagger.

"Guess I'll have to wait until I'm in town," Jagger sighs dramatically.

"Guess you will," I say, and turn to keep walking.

"No, no, wait." Jagger scrambles to the door, staggering a little in his haste. I wrinkle my nose. Jagger's always heading off into the woods on his breaks. I'm not sure how much stuff he smokes, or how he manages to hide it, but he won't be long for the crew if Lincoln catches on. Too bad, too. Lincoln's crew is a sweet deal, even before we got Sierra.

"So the girl," Jagger lowers his voice conspiratorially. "Whatcha think?"

"She's all right," I say. She was more than all right. She's so sweet, the way she cares about us. Most people look at me and see my brother's doppelganger. Not Sierra. She pauses to study me carefully before addressing me by name. Every time.

"I'm trying to figure out where she came from, what her deal is. She say anything?"

I shrug negative.

"A hundred bucks says she was turning tricks in town and approached Lincoln."

I wrinkle my nose. "That doesn't seem like Sierra." There was something about her. A freshness, a spark of joy. I can tell when she dances.

"Come on, bet me."

"No." I step back. "If you need money, go ask Saint for a loan."

"Awww, no," Jagger whines. "He'll throw me out. Right after he turns me down."

I shrug. "Guess that's your answer."

"But seriously." Jagger leans close and I automatically retreat. "Something's up with Sierra. I'm gonna find out. I think she's fucking Lincoln extra."

"You're just annoyed she got the night off tonight."

"I mean, what else does she have to do?" Jagger exclaims and I step back from the spray.

"Leave her alone, Jagger. You got more things to worry about." I point behind him when he looks confused. "You better air out your room better than this. Smells like skunk."

Later, I'm propped in bed. Oren's next to me, sawing wood. You'd think it'd bother me that he snores all night, but we've shared a room forever and I'm just used it.

Tonight, I can't sleep. Jagger's words gnaw at me. *I'm trying to figure out where she came from, what her deal is.* He has me wondering too. Why did Sierra take Lincoln's offer? What was she doing before? Does she have a place to stay? Friends?

I scoff at myself. Stupid. Of course she had a life before this. Lincoln didn't conjure her out of the air. She just seems fragile and delicate, a butterfly dancing around a new stump. Oren calls her a fairy, as if she was a magical creature that might up and disappear.

I'm deep in thought when a shadow darts down the hall. I push out of bed and peek out the door.

"Sierra?"

"Hey," she whispers. She comes close, studying my face. "Elon."

I take her arm and draw her gently inside my room.

Jagger's door is shut, otherwise he would've intercepted her. "Everything okay?"

"I slept all day," she says, regret coloring her voice. "Like, all day. I didn't even wake up to eat."

"You needed your rest." I lift my hands but don't touch her. I feel too big, too clumsy, too dumb to say or do anything.

"Well, now I can't sleep. God what is that noise?"

"Oh..." I half turn so she can see my brother sprawled on the bed. "Oren."

"Is he always like that?"

"Yeah," I answer. "Uh, don't worry about him. He sleeps through anything."

"Sounds like it."

I let out a loud laugh, like an idiot. My lips feel too large for my face. Just being close to her, my heart thumps. Her features are perfect and pixie-like. Her skin glows like she's lit from within.

I'm staring, but I can't stop.

She drags her gaze away from the bed and glances up at me. "What?" she asks, smiling.

"Nothing. You're beautiful," I blurt.

She looks away, biting her lip, before meeting my gaze again boldly. "So are you. What did Jagger say?"

Before jealousy rushes through me she continues, "Jewish mother and Irish dad. What was that like?" she asks.

"I dunno," I say clumsily. "Loud. Lots of shouting."

She cocks her head to the side. "Did you get in trouble a lot?"

"Not me. Oren. He did dumb shit."

"Oooh, did your parents like you better than him?"

"Naw." I can't even meet her dancing gaze. "They didn't

bother to find out who did it. He'd blame me and I'd blame him, and they'd just punish us both."

"Poor you."

I can't help but grin at the humor in her voice.

"So where is home for you, Elon?"

"New York."

"Me too!"

"Really?" I feel a little thrill at having something in common with her.

"Yeah, upstate. Well, my mom was from there. She was a free spirit. Took off and never looked back. My half-brothers are there still, though. I think." Her brow wrinkles.

"You don't know them?"

"Did... did you want to sit down? Just to talk or hang or something?"

She hesitates, her eye catching on Oren's carvings. Just then, my brother lets out a snort, and rolls over, still asleep.

A little laugh gusts from her and she shakes her head. "No. Better not. Don't want to play favorites. Jagger might get jealous."

I hide my own jealousy that she cares so much about Jagger's feelings. That's just Sierra. She cares. "Well, good night."

"Good night, Elon." With a little wave, she's gone.

～

Sierra

"You like teasing us, you fucking slut?" Mason's breath is hot on my ear.

"Oh yeah," I purr. My body goes hot, then cold, desire filling my headspace like hallucinogenic gas. I'm high, pupils dilating as I get another hit of Mason's hate. "I love it."

"You're a bad, bad girl." He grips my wrists harder.

"Yes." I sway my ass, arching my back, seeking contact. He's pinned me to the door, the shackles of his large hands our only point of contact. His body hovers behind me, just out of reach. Every time I brush him, sensation flares through my body. "Yes."

"Take off your skirt." I wore a little black skirt and black bra for Friday night's performance. The guys told me to take the night off, but as soon as lights went out lodge-wide, I found myself sneaking into Mason's room, my whole body quivering in anticipation.

I strip off the skirt and start to turn, but he slams me back against the door. "Face the wall. Don't move."

His fingers trace the curve of my bottom. My whole pussy clenches, begging for him to touch me. My knees go weak and I sway, leaning into his hard strength to keep from sliding into a juicy puddle on the floor.

"Bad girl." He swats my ass again. "You're a bad girl. Say it."

"I'm a bad girl." I bite my lip a second before adding, "I should be punished."

"Oh, I'll punish you." He pulls back and drags me to the bed.

"Hands and knees," he orders. I scramble into position and look back at him expectantly.

Whap! I hiss and jerk forward, away from the punishing palm.

"Back in position." Mason prowls at the foot of the bed like a lion studying his helpless prey. "You do what I say, and take what I give you." His fingers trail over my jean-clad backside and I whimper. "You're gonna take it all."

Yes. Oh, yes. I push back into his palm.

"I'll teach you to flaunt your body in front of the crew, lead us on." He smacks me again and I flinch, but don't jump away. Pain settles in with an edge of excitement I want. He rubs my ass and arousal surges back.

"This belongs to me." Mason squeezes my right cheek hard enough to bring tears to my eyes.

"Just tonight," I whisper.

He growls, low in his throat. "This is mine." His touch softens, soothing me. *Trust me,* his fingers say.

"Yours, Mason." I swallow around the lump in my throat.

He fists a hand in my hair, jerking my head back. "Don't say my name." He drags my lips to his cock. I open my mouth and take him in, gagging a little as he fills my mouth, knocking the back of my throat. His hand searches between my legs. I'm wet, sopping. I hum around the head of his dick like I've discovered a new musical instrument.

"That's it, bitch, take it all." His cock pokes the back of my throat.

I choke and laugh, whipping my head away so I can catch my breath. He's such a cliché, his malice toward me almost a role he plays. I should keep away.

Yet I'm here, on all fours, sucking him like he's a lollipop in my favorite flavor. Mason makes me stupid.

Mason's hand is still knotted in my hair. Once I catch my breath, I roll my eyes. "Been watching a lot of porn, Mason?"

"Shut. The. Fuck. Up." His hand shoots out, hard fingers digging into either side of my throat, squeezing. My brain soars as my limbs clamber against the bed. Arousal bursts in my pussy, driving me higher and higher into the heights of desire.

Then he lets go and I'm falling back to Earth.

"This"—Mason slaps my pussy and the promise of pleasure shocks through me like electricity—"is mine. I own it tonight. I say whether you cum... or not."

"Yes," I agree. Mason is a rough rollercoaster but I enjoy the ride. I sag back into the bed and let him torment me. Fingers, thumbs and mouth come to my pussy until I'm writhing, ready to drag myself over the edge. Little noises escape my throat, but just as pleasure's close enough to snap and spill light into every corner of me, Mason kneels between my splayed legs, pulls my calves to his shoulders, and slams into me, bending me in half. I break on the fifth thrust, and spasm through the rest of his brutal fucking. He grunts and roots deep inside me for his finale, and we stare at each other.

Do you really hate me? I want to ask. Before I get the nerve, his gaze hardens. He drags his cock out of me—I shudder as liquid spills from my opening. I lay there, panting, as he fiddles with something on the dresser. He returns and cleans me up with a cloth, swabbing slowly and refusing to meet my eyes. Somehow this feels more intimate than anything I've ever done with a man.

When he's done, he stands. He's shirtless, his cock jutting out from his open jeans.

"You want me to clean you?" I gesture to his wet crotch.

"No. Get out."

I stumble out of Mason's room for the second time in two days. The door closes behind me and I lean against the wall, squeezing my eyes shut. I wish it was a dream.

It's not a dream.

It's Friday, and Lincoln told me to take the night off. I could do whatever—whoever—I pleased. And after chatting with Elon, I walked right to Mason's door and knocked.

It wasn't totally my fault. I slept most of the day, and dreamt of a large, hard body covering mine. It could've been any of the guys, really. I almost slipped into Lincoln's room, but couldn't bring myself to pass Mason's door.

Fuck, there's something wrong with me.

I head to my room, but halfway there, switch directions.

Saint's light is on. I knock lightly and wait for his deep voice. Cracking the door, I peek through it.

"Sierra."

"You said to wait until Saturday." I bite my lip.

Saint shifts and pats the bed. "Get in here, girl."

I sit on the bed, and he coaxes me close. "Come on. Curl up cozy." His dark eyes sweep over my face a moment. "Cry a little."

When I blink at him, he adds, "Do what you need to do."

I do as he says, taking inventory of my feelings. Is the heaviness in my chest brimming over? Do I need to cry?

I scooch closer to Saint's giant form. Wrapping a large arm around me, he tucks me into his side. Saint tips me back so he can study my face, I settle and sigh.

"Did he hurt you?" he asks gently.

"No." I'm surprised at the sniffle in my voice. "Well, yes, but in a way I liked." I don't ask him how he knows where I was or who I was doing. Saint knows everything. My brain has filed him somewhere between Einstein and God.

Saint keeps his arm around me, frowning thoughtfully at the floor. "He's intense. His girl left him and got pregnant by another man."

I go still, my whole body wrapped around the secret inside me. The baby I now have even more reason to hide. "Fuck."

"You look like her." His arms tighten around me briefly, squeeze reassurance.

I stay quiet a few moments, enjoying his hold. He's a solid wall between me and the world.

"Saint?" I twist so I can see his face. "Have you ever spanked a woman?"

"With my hand or with an implement?" He chuckles at my look of shock. Slowly, as if I'm a wild creature who might bolt, he disentangles us, and heads to the large trunk in the corner. He lifts it without any sign of its weight, and carries it over to me. Watching my face, he opens it.

I bite back a gasp so hard I nearly swallow my tongue .

"When it comes to spanking, nothing wrong with a hand," Saint tells me. "But there's so much more to explore." He rummages in the box while my eyebrows crawl to my hairline.

"Consider this. Which one of these do you think would hurt more?" He lifts a long, inch-thick wooden paddle and a long, thin dowel.

I point to the paddle.

"See, you're wrong. This gives a nice, thuddy sort of pain." He sets the paddle down. "Whereas this," he hefts the dowel. "Stings like a mother." He fingers the end, then slaps his own palm and shows me the red line. "The cane is too intense for a beginner."

"So will you use"—I motion to the box—"any of this on me?"

Saint shuts the box. "Do you want me to?"

I swallow. Slowly I nod.

The bed creaks as he reseats himself facing me. With a long finger, he brushes my hair from my face. "Why?"

"What?"

"Why do you want this?"

I lick my lips, searching for the answer. "I'm not having sex after this," I blurt. A slight flicker of his eyes indicates his surprise. Saint has a pretty good poker face. "I mean, after this gig, I'm going to take a break. From sex and, um"—I wave my hand around vaguely—"men."

A pause ,then he nods as if he understands. I don't question how he takes my meaning. I find it quicker to assume Saint knows everything.

I lean closer, feeling bolder. "Until then, I'm up for anything. I mean, I'd like to try more things."

"Just to be clear, we're talking about you coming to me and doing a scene. A set amount of time where I take you through your paces and use some of these things on you."

I don't look at the trunk. It's too scary. And yet, I have the feeling I'll be fantasizing about Saint slapping that cane down on my skin. "Yes."

A slow smile spreads across Saint's face. He cups my chin. "Saturday."

BLINDFOLDED, I kneel on a pillow before the bed. Behind me, Saint rummages in the trunk. I twitch, cocking my ear toward him, every sense straining for clues of what's to come. The blindfold is soft and snug, and obliterates any light. Funny how such a small scrap of fabric inverts my world.

A whisper of a shadow washes over me and I jump as Saint takes my hand.

"Shhh, girl, easy." He lifts my hand to the bed, running my fingers down a long handle to a mane of soft leather strips. "Feel this." I fondle the velvety strands, my breath rushing in and out. "This is a flogger. This is all I'll use tonight."

"Will it hurt?" My voice sounds very small.

"Not at first. I'll start over your clothes." He brushes my back with the implement. "Give you a chance to get used to it. Then I'll check in. You ready?"

I swallow, twisting my fingers in my lap. Images cram my mind. The flogger doesn't seem too intense, but Saint's a pretty big guy. In his hands, anything can be a weapon.

The silence stretches.

"We don't have to do this," he rumbles.

"I know." More hand twisting. Try as I might, I can't stomach the thought of giving up, pulling the blindfold off, rising and running out the door. It's not that I'm brave, I'm just really, really curious.

Another swallow, then I tell him, "I'm ready."

At first Saint teases me, running the flogger over my shoulders and face, tickling and acclimating me to the sensation. I'm laughing and relaxed by the time he steps behind me, and lets the leather strands wash over my shirt. The flogger falls in an easy rhythm, a gentle, drumming rain soothing me.

"Deep breaths, girl. That's it," Saint murmurs, and lays the leather on a little harder. Between the deep breathing and the heat in my back, my whole body relaxes.

He pauses and I twitch, rising from my trance.

"All good?" he asks and I nod.

My pussy is an ocean. I shift on my knees and he snaps the strands with more force, making me flinch. He backs off, flogging me so lightly it feels like a beautiful massage. The blows increase until the final flick stings.

I let out a little moan/sigh.

"Keep going?"

"Yes," I mumble. My head droops, growing heavier with each impact.

Behind me, Saint chuckles. "You're in a trance."

"Mmmm. Don't stop."

"All right, girl. Hands up."

Languid, floating, I raise my arms and let him slip off my shirt. On his orders, I came without a bra. He brushes the flogger over my sensitized back, the merest touch making my pussy throb and my mouth grow lax. I'm in a pleasure trance: my body primed for touch, my mind a thousand miles away. The flogger strokes my skin like extra-soft fingers. I shiver as the tingling in my pussy intensifies.

"Life is stressful," Saint murmurs. "Sometimes it's nice to give up control. Keep breathing. Good girl." He lays on the flogger, whipping me lightly up and down. I've melted forward; he pauses to guide me closer to the bed. I lift my arms and stretch them out over the blanket. He flogs up and down my sides, careful blows wrapping the strands around to reach my small breasts. I suck in a breath, but the sensation never rises above the barest sting. Tears well in my eyes as I imagine Saint's size, the flogger a tiny toy in his great hand, laying the flogger down with such care on my narrow back.

I sink further into a warm darkness, a safe place. I'm floating here, my body suspended in a pool of sensation. I hope I'll drift forever. All my problems seem so far away.

"Sierra." Saint's hand cups the back of my neck and I realize the flogging has stopped. My whole body pulses with the memory of each blow.

"Huh," I sigh, surfacing. "Everything okay?"

"That's my line." He chuckles, a delicious, dark-chocolatey sound. "You with me?"

"I'm here." I'm practically drooling. "That was awesome."

"We're not done." His large hand slides under my arm,

lifting me. "Up and lie down on the bed. On your back. Good girl."

I press my palms to the bedspread, my breath catching in my chest. Saint props my feet apart, widening my knees and baring the crotch of my jeans. As soon as I realize what he's about, my hands fist the blanket.

"Shhh." He drapes the flogger's strands between my legs, softly thrumming my pussy through the thick denim. "I'll be gentle. You trust me?"

"Um. Okay. Yeah."

"You want the blindfold off?"

I think about it. It's nice to drown in darkness. "No."

"All right. Relax." The flogger brushes my jean-clad legs, tickling my inner thighs. My pussy fills with juice. I grit my teeth, digging my nails into the bed, planting my heels and trying not to push up into the soft blows. Saint uses the flogger to deliver the lightest butterfly brushing sensation. He swings the strands back and forth, painting desire on my pussy. My legs tremble.

"Knees apart," Saint orders. "Don't make me tell you again."

Oh god. A plea wells up in my throat, escaping as a needy groan.

"You like when I boss you around, girl?"

My pussy screams *Yes* but my mind screams *No*. I open my mouth and lick my lips.

"You don't have to answer." Saint's voice bubbles from the subterranean depths. "Just let go. I got you." The flogger resumes its drumming beat between my legs. I grip the sheets in earnest, need rising in me. Tears leak out of the corners of my eyes. Without meaning too, I begin to moan. The sound reaches my ears and I cut it out.

"It's all right, girl. Let it out."

"I'm scared." The words escape without check. My mind's on leave, on vacation, out to lunch. Someone's driving my body but it's not me.

Saint pauses, cups my knee. "You feeling out of control?"

"Yes." I have to search for speech.

"You ready to stop?"

My muscles clench. "No," I whisper, and say again louder. "No, don't stop." Several moments pass before I add, "Please."

"Good girl." Saint trails the strands between my legs. My body strains for the slightest sensation. "I could make you cum, just like this," he murmurs. "It wouldn't take much. Just a little more force."

My hips jerk, begging.

"Or I could put the flogger away. Do you think you deserve to cum?"

The question makes me start. *Yes,* I want to cry out. But I'm not in control. "I've been good."

"Have you?" Saint pushes my knees wider. "It might take quite a few forceful strikes. I don't know if you can bear it."

I swallow hard, because I don't know either.

"No," he says. "I think I'll go easy on you. Lie still."

The bed creaks as he sits beside me. Cool fingers trail over my bare midriff and slip into my jeans. He finds me wet and soaking, quivering.

"Such a sweet little pussy." He hooks one finger inside me, probing, exploring. I hold my breath. "So greedy." My inner muscles clench. "It's not going to take much, is it? Just a little... touch." He strokes along my clit and I tense, pushing my body up to meet his questing hand. "On my word, you're going to cum for me."

A whimper. *Yes.* A tremor runs through me. He moves

his finger and flicks just the spot. My head jerks back, a gasp bursting in my ears.

"Yes. There. Cum for me, girl." The slightest movement, so small, so perfect, and I break, hips snapping, legs trembling. I lie, weak and happy, as he paints my lips with my own wetness. When he's done, I lick my lips. "Good girl."

Saint peels the blindfold off and I blink, re-entering the world reluctantly. He moves to return the flogger to the trunk.

"Wait," I mumble, clearing my throat. "You're not gonna fuck me?"

"No, girl." He pushes the trunk back against the wall, gives it a little pat before turning to me. "You gotta earn it."

My lower lip pushes out in a blatant pout. It says, *Please?*

Saint's broad shoulders move with a huge sigh. "On your knees." He jerks his chin. I sink back onto the pillow.

He takes himself in hand, tugging, palming the head, his hand jerks faster.

"Touch yourself," he orders, and I sink my fingers into my wetness, frigging frantically.

"Stop," he barks. And I do, gritting my teeth as I obey. My pussy throbs as Saint strokes himself off. Staring at his cock, sweat breaks out over my body I want him inside me, so bad. But if I haven't earned that, I want his cum.

With a shudder and a sigh, Saint cums in his hand.

Offers it to me—a pool of white.

I don't know what takes hold of me. It was like I was someone else. I seize his wrist and bring it close so I can lap at it with my tongue, a kitten with milk. I clean every inch of his palm.

"Stand up, girl." He helps me rise, then shoves his sticky hand in my jeans, cupping my pussy and thumbing my clit until my orgasm snaps and floods my body with pleasure.

WEEKS PASS. I mark the days off my calendar in a rotation of men: Lincoln, Jagger, Elon and Oren, Mason, Saint. They are my days and nights and dreams.

Each man is an acquired taste. Even the twins have differences that give our lovemaking a distinct flavor. Elon comes into me carefully, his blue eyes wide as if the moment is too good to be true. Oren is more methodical, as if I'm a puzzle he can carefully prise apart and put back together better than before. They even have a different scent: Elon smells like pine and fresh air, Oren of sawdust, both delicious. When they come home covered in mud, I greet them gleefully, hugging them, pulling them close to suck in lungfuls of air. They protest I'm getting all dirty and I wink, suggesting we can shower together. I enjoy watching the scarlet creep up their freckled necks.

On my night off, I hang around in the dining hall and play checkers and strip poker with Jagger and the twins. Jagger usually invites me back to his room to drink and smoke a doobie. He reminds me of Jack—a carefree soul. The reminder hurt, which is why I always turned Jagger's invitations down. That, and I was pregnant.

Saint took it upon himself to complete my education. He gave me stacks of books to read, mostly classic, but a fair number of romance novels too (I couldn't read murder mysteries or thrillers anymore without nightmares). Lincoln showed me his logs and maps and old forestry textbooks. Even Roy and Tommy befriended me, inviting me to their room to listen to their music. I floated from room to room, listening and learning and living with these men.

And at night I fucked them. Slow fucking, fun fucking,

double team, hate fucking and dominance submission scenes.

THESE WERE the times when I was present to myself, when I could give up the worry and weight of what was to come. In the late hours of the night, I gave myself to the men, and in return, they gave me a space to just be. I surrender my body, and they seduce my mind.

But I'm careful, so careful, not to risk my heart.

7

Sierra

I sit at the table alone, alert to the sounds coming from the kitchen. I'm alone in the lodge with Saint, on one of his random days off. The scent of bacon drifts my way, I grip my fork and fight tears of happiness. I love bacon.

"Awww, yes," I moan when Saint sets a full plate down in front of me. As soon as it touches the table, I'm shoveling food in my open mouth. I start with eggs so I can sate my greedy body before savoring the bacon. I'm grateful when Saint leaves the room for a moment to give me and my plate some alone time.

When he comes back out to hover over me, I've managed to slow down. I've abandoned my fork and use my fingers to carefully prise apart the bacon, tasting each piece and giving it its own special treatment. I let the fat melt in my mouth, crunch the hard bits, lick my fingers to clean them from grease. There's something so present, so tactile about eating with my hands. A full sensory experience.

Then I catch a glimpse of Saint's face as he watches me and realize I'm an animal.

Clearing my throat, I push away from the table and wipe my hands on a napkin, effectively rejoining civilization.

Saint looks at me, then my plate, then me. "You need to eat more," he rumbles.

"You always say that." I break off a piece of cornbread and pop it into my mouth.

"And more water." Saint plunks a glass down to the right side of my plate. "Less coffee." He plucks my mug out of my hand.

"Hey!" I protest, but he shakes a long finger at me and strides off. I consider running after him and tackling him, but the effect would be like a mouse attacking a mountain. Saint could swat me like a mosquito, and we both know it.

So I sit and finish my breakfast, drinking the water in sips so I don't drown the contents of my stomach. When the plate is clean, I push back, my hands on my stomach bump. If Saint looks, he'll just think I have a food baby.

"Eat up, little one," I whisper. "Grow big and strong." I drift in a food coma, jolting awake with a smile when I feel tiny flutters inside. My baby is moving around.

It's been a pretty good pregnancy so far. The nausea is gone, thank fuck, but I'm still tired at random moments. Some days I forget I'm pregnant, others I bite my lip to keep from whining and telling everyone.

A chair scrapes the floor and Saint settles in beside me. He sets three plates of food down and eats methodically. He doesn't appear to rush, but the food disappears at a rapid pace.

When he's half done with the third plate, he slows and rests his left hand on the back of my neck.

"You feeling okay?" he asks. His finger swirls the hair at the nape of my neck and my body stirs with interest.

"Oh yeah." I fake calm. "We gonna scene tonight?" I try to keep my voice casual but lean forward, my body swaying toward him like a flower to the sun.

"Is that what you want?"

"Yes, please." I'm breathless, blood charging to my cheeks and pussy, making me hot and flushed.

Saint takes a minute to regard me. "We'll have to stop the rough stuff soon."

I sit up straighter. "What? Why? I just got to the point where I crave it."

"I don't want to hurt you."

"You can't hurt me. You make it feel good."

"I don't know how much you can take, with the baby and all."

Record scratch. I open and close my mouth, suddenly dizzy. Saint stares at me. I can't look away, even though I don't want to meet his eyes

"You know?" I whisper.

Keeping his hand on the back of my neck, Saint takes a sip of his coffee. "I can tell when a woman's breeding."

I put my hands over my softly bloated belly as if to hide it. "I've been gaining weight..." I stall.

Saint sets down his coffee and turns. He hovers a large hand over my belly. He could cover the whole thing with one hand. "That's not fat. That's a baby bump."

Now I can't meet his eyes. "I didn't know how to tell you."

"You need to tell them."

"You gonna tell?" I can barely get the words out.

"Not my secret to tell. It's yours." With that, he gets up and clears the table, leaving me huddled in my seat, numb. The food I just ate is heavy as a rock.

When he returns, I haven't moved. My eyes feel scratchy. "Saint, I didn't know. I didn't know when I took the job."

He stares at me, back to the impassive blankness that tells me nothing of what he's thinking. I want to cry and scream. I want to beg him to let me keep my secret for a little longer, at least until I know where I can go to save myself and my baby.

Maybe it'll work out. Maybe Lincoln won't be mad, and he'll let me stay until the season's over. Maybe the money and time will be enough to get me south, beyond the reach of the Hell Riders.

Yeah right.

"What are you going to do?" Saint asks, and my heart sinks. His tone is thoughtful, but distant. No trace of warmth.

I hug my middle. "I don't know."

I LAY in my bed the rest of the day. Saint leaves me alone, thank fuck. Evening falls and the lodge fills with the noise of the woodsmen, boots stomping, voices shouting, showers cutting on and off.

I roll to my side and hug my pillow. *You need to tell them.* What will Lincoln say? Mason? There's no way they'll let me stay.

"Sierra?" Jagger calls from my door. He raps softly. "You feeling okay?"

"Fine," I croak, glad my back is to the door

"Dinner's ready."

"I'm not hungry. I'll be out... after." I squeeze my eyes shut until he leaves. Then I press my fist against my mouth and try not to burst into tears.

I'm tempted to grab my clothes and stuff them in my old backpack. Slip out the back and start walking. Maybe I can hitchhike somewhere decent, live on the streets until it gets cold.

My body contracts around the pillow just imagining it. Who am I kidding? I bet everything on this gig. I rise and brush my hair with shaking hands. Maybe I can convince Lincoln to let me stay to the end of the season. I'll clean, cook, help with kitchen duty—whatever. Jagger and the twins will probably still want me. Lincoln—no way. This will be a breach of trust for him. I told him I could do the job and I lied. Besides, like Saint, Lincoln won't feel comfortable using a pregnant woman. It was hard enough to get them to accept me as an equal partner in the bedroom.

Mason—he might get off on the situation. Didn't his last girl cheat on him and get pregnant? I might appeal to him on the basis that this is an opportunity for revenge. Of course, the best revenge would be kicking me out.

Not Mason, then. Fuck.

I toss down the brush, pick up my mascara, and put that down too. Don't really want to draw attention to my red eyes. And even the most waterproof mascara won't hold up to a good ugly cry. I don't want raccoon eyes.

My stomach stutters as I open my door. If I'm lucky, I won't throw up. Awesome. Won't that convince them to let me say.

The chorus of men's voices swells to greet me as I enter the mess hall. They fall to a low murmur as I approach.

"Sierra? Are you all right?" Lincoln frowns. He half rises, and I put out my hand to stop him.

"I have a confession to make." My voice echoes in the big space with my oracle-like proclamation. Forehead creasing, Lincoln sits.

I swallow. "I have something to tell you." I hesitate, my gaze snagging on Saint's. The big guy leans against the wall in the back. He meets my eyes and nods slowly. "I'm pregnant."

Silence. Most of the guys wait motionless, as if I haven't said anything. Roy and Tommy exchange glances.

Elon raises his hand. I point to him like I'm a kindergarten teacher.

"Is it mine?" he asks, all innocent blue eyes.

I melt a little. "No," I say gently. "I was pregnant when I got here."

Nobody says anything. I splay my hands as if to offer reasons, excuses, but my hands are empty. I've got nothing.

"Well... this is unexpected," Jagger drawls. He doesn't look annoyed or upset. The twins' eyes dart around, as if waiting to see what everyone else does. Mason stares at the floor.

Lincoln's chair scrapes as he pushes away from the table. "No dancing tonight. Sierra's off."

"But it's my—" Jagger starts.

"I said no," Lincoln snaps. He clamps a hand on the back of my neck and propels me toward his room, holding me like a bear who's caught a kitten by the scruff. The fear in my stomach threatens to boil over.

Inside his room, I shrink toward the bed.

"Sit," Lincoln orders. He stays standing, filling the room with his height and muscle and black-bearded scowl. I realize my hands have automatically covered my stomach. I pull them back, noting miserably that Lincoln is glaring at my belly.

"How far along?" he grinds out.

"I'm almost halfway."

"The father?"

Dead. "Out of the picture."

Lincoln starts pacing the room. "Did he hurt you?"

"What?" I shake my head a little because I don't think I properly heard the question.

Lincoln looms over me, hair tangled, eyes wild. "The man who did this to you. Did he hurt you?"

My mouth flaps open a moment before I say, "No. We were together. We were young and stupid and had sex without a condom, but he didn't hurt me." Something like a growl escapes from Lincoln's throat. "He's not the reason I'm running," I add quietly.

Lincoln resumes pacing and my eyes track him from one corner of the room to the other. "What about family? Do they know you're here?"

"No. I mean, I don't have any." That's not entirely true. Like I'd mentioned to Elon, I have two half-brothers in the lower forty-eight Lynny mentioned a few times, but I've never met them and they don't know about me.

He rubs his hand over his jaw, mussing his beard. "No mom or dad? Nobody?"

"My mom's dead," I bite out. "I don't know who my dad is. Lynny never told me."

"Lynny?"

"My mom." I rub my belly. Poor little bump won't know Jack, either.

"All right." Lincoln paces back and forth, the room growing smaller with every pass. "All right. What about friends, someone you trust—"

"Why are you asking this?" I rise from the bed to put my hands on my hips. "What is your problem?"

"My problem?" Lincoln stops. "You're twenty-one. You're all alone. You're pregnant—"

"So what's it to you?"

"I care about you," he roars so loud the door rattles. He reaches for me, checks himself, and lowers his hands gently to my shoulders. "Your problems are mine too."

I bite my lip.

"Sierra—"

"You're wrong. It is my problem. Mine alone."

"Oh yeah? What are you going to do?" His hand flies out toward the window. "Leave?"

"If you want," I whisper. He jerks like I struck him.

"You think I want you to leave?" He rushes to me and I wince, but he just kneels and takes my hands, chafing them. "You think I wouldn't help?"

I shrug, unable to answer. Tears well up and spill in twin rivulets down my face.

Lincoln curses gruffly, and pulls me forward. "Come here." His body is warm and solid, the shirt soft. I bury my face against him and sob. He just holds me.

"Fuck, Sierra," Lincoln mutters, a hand on my head to keep me close. "You're not alone."

I step back and sniffle. My face is a mess of snot and tears, but at least I don't have raccoon eyes. It takes me a few tries to find my voice. "I'm not?" I hiccup.

"No," Lincoln tells me. His big bear arms flex around me.

A pounding on the door makes me jump away.

"Enter," Lincoln says, a half a second after the door opens. Mason plants himself in the doorway, jaw clenched. His face darkens when he sees my tear-stained face. I stare back, dully. I don't have the energy to deal with his moodiness.

"Everything all right?" he asks Lincoln, his eyes on me.

"Everything's fine," I smile and wipe my eyes so I'm more convincing. "We were just... working some things out."

"She's not going anywhere. You're not kicking her out." Mason squares off with Lincoln, folding his arms over his chest. He's not as tall as the crew chief, but every inch of him is muscle. His body screams, *Try and stop me.*

I sway a little. Did Mason just defend me? I hope I fall on the bed if I faint from surprise.

"You think I'd—" Lincoln notices my wobbling and puts an arm around me. Deep breaths widen his barrel chest. "No." His voice is about an octave deeper. "I'm not sending her away. Sierra belongs here." His arm tightens. "With us."

Mason stares at me a moment, his eyes boring holes into my face. He steps back, still looking angry, nods once and stomps out, slamming the door.

I let out a sigh, slumping against Lincoln. He brushes his lips over my forehead and guides us to the bed, where he sits with his back against the headboard and pulls me into his arms. His large hands cradle one of mine, hovering over my belly. I angle myself to face him, tug up my shirt and lay his left and right palms over the gentle bulge. His fingers spread across my taut skin, barely touching me, as if holding a bubble he doesn't want to pop. I put my hands over his and press, and he lets out a shaky breath. Once he's holding my belly, really holding me, I let out a sigh.

"Why didn't you tell me?" he murmurs, gaze on my belly.

"I didn't know. Not until the doctor. Then I thought you would kick me out. I know better now," I add quickly, when his eyes go wild again. "But this is no place for a child."

His hands are so large they cover most of my baby bump. His finger stroke along my sides. "What's your plan?"

I swallow a hysterical laugh. "Live here until the season

ends. Dance every night, and fuck whoever wants me. When it's over... take the money and try to survive."

"You didn't think you could ask me for help?" his tone accuses.

I wanted to. I bite my lip.

"Well?" For a moment his bitter dark eyes remind me of Mason's.

"I didn't know. I'm sorry. I didn't want to assume..."

Lincoln's hands leave my bump, landing on my shoulders and turning me so I'm back to his front, fully locked in his arms. His beard tickles the back of my neck, and his biceps bulge on either side of me. He squeezes once, hard, and I settle. The hard mass of knots in my chest unravel.

We sit like that for a long moment, my breathing slowing to match his. I could curl up and go right to sleep like this, hibernate like a little bear in the shelter of a strong man's arms.

Just when I'm about to doze off, Lincoln's lips find my ear. "Sierra. Don't you get it? I found you. I'm keeping you."

Oren

MY SMALL KNIFE digs into the smooth wood a mere milliliter from my thumb. A long slow, stroke and then I realize I'm wearing a 'whittling frown'. What my brother calls my expression when I'm concentrating. I smooth it out quickly, in case someone walks by and wonders whether I'm upset.

It's been two hours since Sierra made her announcement, and a lot of people are upset. Not Roy and Tommy—they disappeared into their room after helping clean up dinner. Lincoln's still with Sierra. He left his room long enough to ask for a plate of food. Saint delivered it and the two of them talked quietly in the hall before Lincoln ducked inside, plate in hand. There was a small fight when Jagger confronted Saint, insisting that he wanted to see Sierra, but Jagger stopped when Mason told him off. Now they're all at opposite ends of the dining hall, sitting or brooding or puttering around, as if Sierra will pop out any minute and tell them it was all a joke. I got sick of the dirty looks an hour ago, and retreated to my room.

I'm not really mad. I don't think anyone is, except maybe Jagger. He's horn-gry, horny/angry, because he thought tonight was his turn with Sierra. Looks like that little arrangement is over. I don't mind. I'll miss the sex, sure, but I don't mind too much. If she left entirely, I'd miss the sex, but I'd miss her more.

Down the hall, the shower turns off. A minute later, my brother tromps into the room, wearing nothing but a towel. He leaves the door open as he dries off and gets dressed.

"Whatcha making?" Elon asks.

I shrug. Michelangelo described sculpting as a *'forza di levare'*. A process of taking away. He saw a block of marble and removed everything that was not his sculpture. I think of wood carving the same way. There's a figure inside this piece of pine. If I sit here and shave off enough, it'll reveal itself to me.

Some people have special knives and order premium wood for wood carvings. I like being able to carve with whatever I have on hand. A bit of pine and a pocket knife. There's always enough wood around here. I collect it. In the off-season, I sell premium blocks of wood on Etsy to wood carving enthusiasts. I even got a little camera to record me whittling something start to finish, to show my technique.

My videos on YouTube are pretty popular—especially the dog and elephant carvings. Saint said he'll teach me how to put up a paywall and turn the videos into a course this winter.

The bed creaks as Elon sits down. He's quiet for a while, but I know he wants to talk. I could ask him a question, but if I wait long enough, he'll open up.

Finally, he scratches his head and asks, "You want kids?"

I look at him like he's crazy. "Yeah."

"How many?"

I shrug. "However many my woman wants." My knife reaches the end of the piece and a nice long wood shaving curls and drops off into the pile at my feet.

Elon sighs. I keep carving, sensing his gaze on my hands. I want to turn away, hide my creation as if too fragile to be seen.

"What about Sierra? Would you want kids with her?" he asks.

I pause for a moment. My dick jerks at the thought of holding Sierra, laying her down and pressing inside her. Her skin is like the smoothest marble, a warm and living sculpture, each dip and curve perfect under my hands. What would it be like to watch her body change and belly grow, knowing all the time it was my seed that took root inside her?

"Yes," I say. "Yes, I'd want children with Sierra. If she'd have me."

Elon sighs again. "Me too." He fidgets and I go back to carving. I used to fidget as much as he did, before I started carving.

"Lincoln says she's staying here, until she has the baby. Maybe longer." Elon scratches his beard. "He and Saint are talking about whether they should get a place in town, or take her south. They're gonna support her."

I nod my approval. "I'll help."

"Me too," Elon says quickly. "She'll need lots of things for the baby. Diapers, bottles, baby clothes. Lots of them. It gets cold around here in the winter. We should get lots of warm things for the baby. I'll tell Lincoln." My brother stands and crosses to the window, where several of my carvings sit on the ledge. A moose, a dog, an elephant. A little fairy girl, with nimble wings. He nudges that one with a finger. "Sweaters and socks and blankets," he mumbles. "And hats. We lose most of our heat through our heads. That's why babies always should wear hats." He picks up the fairy carving, and it disappears into his big hand. I bite back a reminder for him to be careful. That carving is his favorite. I should give it to him, but first I want to make another, for me.

"Baby hats," Elon muses, looking out the window, still holding the fairy. "Maybe I should learn to knit."

Sierra

"THAT'S THE HAND. See it waving?" the doctor asks.

I nod, even though I don't. The ultrasound looks like an alien landscape, a black and white TV screen filled with static.

"What does that mean?" Lincoln asks softly. He's at my side, holding my hand as the doctor presses his instrument into my belly, maneuvering around to give us a good glimpse of my child.

"One more angle to be sure," the doctor murmurs. He squeezes more goo onto my exposed belly. I suck in a breath.

"Does it hurt?" Lincoln dips his head to mine, lines creasing his forehead. Since my announcement, he's been extra attentive.

"No," I squeeze his hand tighter. "Just cold."

"Heartbeat, one hundred and forty," the doctor announces.

"Is that okay?" Lincoln looks alarmed.

"Oh yes. Well within normal range."

Lincoln and I both take a deep breath and let it out.

"Everything looks good. And you say you want to know the gender?"

I nod and squeeze Lincoln's hand tighter.

"Congratulations," the doctor says. "It's a girl."

Saint

THE WIND NIPS my cheeks as I lean against the truck. Beside me, Elon mimics my pose. His brother sits in the truck bed, whittling with a small pocket knife. He's always carving something. The way Elon twitches with energy, I wish he would mimic his twin and find something to occupy his hands. The rest of the guys have gone to the general store. I did my run earlier in the week, so this trip was unnecessary. When Sierra timidly mentioned that this doctor's appointment was when she'd learn the baby's gender, suddenly everyone found a reason to come to town at the same time.

"What do you think? Boy or girl?" Elon asks.

I shrug. Tonight, Lincoln and I will sit Sierra down, and

tell her our plan. We were going to support her, as long as she needed. By now she should know she was special to us. Maybe she'd choose to stay with us, maybe not, but we hoped she would think about making a life with us, for her baby.

"How long have they been in there?" Oren drifts over, tucking his knife and whittling into his pocket.

I shrug again and grit my teeth as the twins keep asking stupid questions.

"Is everything all right? When will they be done?"

"Guess we'll find out," I say with a glance at the doctor's sign. We'll have to figure out how to get Sierra close to town when she's due, otherwise one of us might have to catch the baby.

"Everything's fine. Lincoln's in there with her," I remind the twins before they get too wound up. The crew leader insisted on going in, his hand on Sierra's slight back, fatherly responsibility written all over him. I bet he'll put his name on the birth certificate, if Sierra lets him.

Oren settles, taking out his carving again. Elon walks up and down the length of the car. I bite my tongue to keep from snapping at him. Instead, I keep an eye on the gas station next to us. A few motorcycles roll in and out, more coming than going, until the lot is full with row upon row of leather and chrome.

"Hey," Jagger shouts as he approaches. The rest of the guys follow, Mason bringing up the rear. "Any word?"

I shake my head silently just as Jagger's eyes snag on someone behind me.

"They're done," Elon announces needlessly as Lincoln guides Sierra down the wheelchair ramp. Her belly has just started to push her shirt out. She looks pale, but gives us a smile.

"Well?" the twins demand, circling her. She looks up at us; she has to look up at all of us, but has no trouble standing up for herself. "Did you find out?"

"Yes," Lincoln answers with infuriating vagueness. "Step back," he warns the guys sharply when they crowd Sierra.

"It's all right," she says. Her soft voice hides her strong will. "It's a girl."

Jagger picks her up and spins her around, whooping over Lincoln's protests. When he sets her down, the twins, and even Roy and Tommy line up for hugs. Mason lurks at the foot of the truck.

"Hey, you want to eat here?" Jagger jerks a thumb at the diner attached to the gas station. "I heard some good things about the place. The parking lot is full."

"Yeah," Lincoln says distractedly. "Go get us a table?"

Sierra is showing the twins a picture of the ultrasound. When she raises her arm, her sleeves slips down to show a few Band-Aids.

I slip to her side. "Everything good?"

"Oh yeah," she laughs when I touch her arm. "They just took blood. Everything's fine. The baby, me—everyone."

"Good." I catch Lincoln's eye. We need to discuss plans sooner rather than later.

We start across the lot toward the restaurant, more motorcycle engines rip the air.

"Lotta bikers around lately," Elon says.

Sierra's steps falter. Her shoulders hunch and she turns, even as the guys stream forward, blocking her from view.

I signal Lincoln and we both watch Sierra shrink into herself, tucking her head and letting her hair fall over her face. She folds in half, hunching over her tiny baby bump, and skittering to a stop before she passes the line of motorcycles.

I'm across the lot before the bikers look up and notice her. My shadow stretches over her.

"Hey," one of the bikers calls. I ignore him. Not a lot of black men this far north. But a man has to be sure before he picks a fight with a guy my size.

In the glass of the diner's door, I watch Lincoln herd Sierra back to the truck. Once she's safely out of sight, I stick my head in to call to the rest of the crew. "Guys. Jagger. We're out."

"But I thought we were getting food—" Jagger turns with surprise on his face.

"Do what you want." I turn on my foot in disgust and head back toward the truck. The bikers don't call at me again, but I feel their malice with every step I take. They want to pick a fight.

Lincoln meets me halfway.

"What's going on?" I keep heading toward the truck.

"Don't know. She just looks scared."

I curse under my breath, looking back at the bikers.

"Take her back," Lincoln says. "You've attracted attention." He nods to the row of bikers who stand in a line, smoking cigarettes and squinting at me.

"They've just never seen a black man in person," I scoff.

"Yeah, well, they might want to do more than look. Hell Riders control this territory. They're probably passing through, collecting protection money."

"Or looking for someone."

"Yeah. Get her out of here." Lincoln hands me the keys. "I'll round up the rest of the boys, distract them. She's scared outta her mind. Soon she'll tell us the truth."

Sierra says nothing as I get inside the truck. She's slid all the way down in the seat, shrunk into the depths of her hoodie. If anyone looks in the passenger seat, they'll see a hoodie and nothing else. I remain silent as she hunkers down. Her teeth chatter a little, even though it's not that cold.

I wait to say something after we pull out of town. A few miles out, she sits up a little, peers out the window. Her fingernails, picking the end of her sweatshirt, are bitten down to the quick.

"Baby daddy was a Rider." I keep my eyes on the road.

"Yeah," she whispers, fear flickering in her expression. It's all I can do to keep on the road, keep from turning around and picking a fight with those bikers. I'd leave half of them unconscious.

I reach out and set my hand on her knee. She's so small my hand completely covers it. "We're not letting anything happen to you."

She jerks her head in the affirmative. I squeeze to be sure she understands.

"Lincoln and I made you a promise. The rest of the guys support it, but it only needs one of us to carry it out. You have nothing to be afraid of. We're gonna give you everything you need, even after you have this baby."

"I know," she says softly. "Thank you."

"And if anyone threatens you, he deals with us." I watch her go rigid out of the corner of my eye and take my hand away. I couldn't help the intense turn of my voice. There's someone out there who's a danger to Sierra. When I find out who, he will cease to walk the earth. It's only a matter of time.

I force myself to sound calm. "It's all right. You're safe. You're with us now."

I hold my breath until she nods. She's with me. One day she'll open up to me or Lincoln, and we'll help her. Lincoln warned me off scaring her.

"Good girl," I praise her. "As long as you know that." As I turn onto the single lane highway, I feel her relax, and add, "I don't let a man mess with what's mine."

∾

Sierra

SAINT and I got to the lodge well before anyone else. He made me eat a sandwich and drink a glass of milk, hovering over me while I ate. I got the feeling he would've chewed it up for me and fed it to me like a momma bird if I refused. After the meal, he brought me to his room, handed me a chocolate bar and a book with a soft pink and white cover. It was written by a midwife, he explained, and had lots of good advice and birthing stories. I only had to page through it for a minute to realize he was right.

After which I promptly lay down on his bed and passed out in a chocolate coma. I couldn't help it. No matter how much I sleep in, after lunch my eyelids close for at least an hour. I complained to Saint and he said the baby was exerting its will on me.

Voices woke me up, rising, falling, arguing. The men were home.

Rubbing my eyes, I pad into the hall. The guys stand in a knot between the table and the door, a circle of angry bearded faces

"I just think—" Jagger is saying, and Lincoln steps into his space, grabbing a piece of paper out of the blond's hand.

"It's none of our business," the crew chief growls. "She'll tell us when she's ready."

"What are you guys talking about?" My voice falls like a grenade between them.

Lincoln, Mason, Saint turn to gaze at me. Elon and Oren look guilty.

"Here." Jagger tugs the piece of paper from Lincoln's hand and holds it out to me. I cross to him and halt, able to recognize the image from a few feet away. It's an old photo of me. A 'missing' poster. With my face on it.

Blood drains out of my face. "Where did you get that?"

"It was hanging on a bulletin board at the diner."

"There's a reward," Jagger points out. "Ten thousand dollars. We could call them and collect it."

I'm shaking my head before he finishes the sentence. "No. No." The Hell Riders must have posted it. Dex knows I was there when Jack died. He's smart—you don't get to run a club like the Hell Riders if you don't have brains. Dex has the perfect combination of brains, drive and utter ruthlessness. *Call her inside, Jack. It's time to share.* If he wants me, there's nothing that will stop him.

Jagger is talking again, waving the poster. I hear nothing over the rushing in my ears. I need to run, hide. Lincoln faces me, lips moving. He wants to know what's wrong. I shake my head. My brain is frozen, racing like a scared rodent. Try as I might, I can't stammer out a clear answer or explanation.

Mason shoves Jagger in disgust. "Put it away."

"But—" Jagger protests.

"Do it," Lincoln commands. "You see it's making her upset." His broad chest fills my vision, and then I'm in his arms, clinging to his thermal as if I can draw strength from the muscles underneath.

Behind us, the circle of guys is breaking. "Ten thousand dollars," Jagger whines and Mason spews profanity. A shout goes up, broken by Saint's rumble, telling them to leave me be.

Then Lincoln is lifting me. "Shhh, it's okay," he murmurs. I curl against his chest, my face hiding under his beard, breathing in the scent of cedar and lemony soap. The snarl of male voices recedes. A door shuts and Lincoln sits on the bed. His hand rubs large circles on my back. With each pass, the ringing in my ears recedes a bit. I'm panting a little, my fingers digging into him. I ease my grip and look at him, unable to force a smile.

"It's all right," he tells me gravely. "You're safe here."

The words bounce off my brain. My wide-eyed stare says, *I don't know what you're telling me.*

Lincoln reads my unspoken confusion. "Saint and I talked." He squeezes my legs, massaging them as he explains. "We want you to stay here until the baby is born, and afterwards. We'll help you. You don't have to worry about working or doing anything for us..."

I drop my head to his chest, unable to hold up its weight. Lincoln stops talking. He holds me, stroking my back and squeezing my tight muscles with strong, gentle hands.

"You can talk to me." Lincoln says. "Anytime. You know that."

I blow out a breath and nod against the firm plate of his pec. His hands keep massaging me. They tell me: *Shh. It's okay. Whenever you're ready.*

"We're with you, whatever you decide," he adds. "We're not going to let anything happen to you."

8

S ierra

FOR THE NEXT FEW DAYS, I lay low. I leave my room for
showers and meals, choosing times when the guys are gone
and the lodge is empty. Jagger and Elon try in vain to coax
me out. After a few days, they stop, and I bet Lincoln and
Saint told them to back off. I stay in bed, with a book, and
stare out the window.

I think a lot about what Lincoln said. How he and Saint
will make a place for me and the baby. I believe they want to
help, but what sort of life could we have out here? A woman
and baby with a lumberjack crew. What would it mean?
What would be my relationship with them? Even if I can be
sure the Hell Riders won't find me and rain down revenge
on everyone who helped me hide, I can't believe all the guys
would be comfortable giving room and board to me indefi-

nitely. Not when I'm a single mom, and not just a convenient piece of ass.

But I don't really know what the guys are thinking. I'm too afraid to leave my room and find out.

One afternoon, I'm lying in bed, stroking my stomach when my door flies open and Mason stomps in. I scramble up, my hair tumbling around my face and shoulders, but he doesn't look at me.

"Here." He slams something down on the dresser so hard it rattles. "You need to take these." After shooting a glare into each corner of the room, he leaves.

I wait until the door slams behind him before going to examine his gift. A bottle of prenatal pills. My heart twists and I struggle to swallow or take a breath. I bring the bottle to my mouth and press the cap to my lips.

Some guys bring chocolate or flowers. Trust Mason to say 'I'm sorry' with a necessary daily dose of folic acid.

That night I leave my room for the first time in a week, and head to the dining room. The guy's chatter falls to a murmur as I approach. The bearded faces hold lots of speculative looks, but when I get close, Saint pushes a chair out for me so I can sit.

"Thank you," I say. As soon as my butt hits the chair, Oren is handing me a plate, Roy is passing the biscuits, and Mason shoves the butter my way. I keep quiet and focus on my plate, but can't help a small smile.

Maybe we can make this work after all.

~

"IT'S BEEN QUIET LATELY," Jagger says, glancing from the road to me. "Nights aren't the same without you."

Fiddling with the zipper on my jacket, I flash him a

smile. My clothes fit tighter now. I'm so used to hiding my body under sweaters and sweatshirts, it was a shock to see my belly pooching out from under my small t-shirts.

The guys didn't say anything, but within the hour Lincoln asked me if I'd pick Saint up some things at the general store. "Buy some things for yourself, while you're at it. Anything you need." He handed me a bank card and had me memorize his pin, but before I left, Tommy came over to hug me, and slipped me a few twenties.

Jagger offered to drive, maybe to make up for scaring me with the wanted poster, or just to get some time alone with me, I didn't know. But I was grateful. The guys were going out of their way to be sweet.

"You doing okay?" Jagger asks, interrupting my thoughts. I realize I'm rubbing my belly and stop.

"Yeah. Everything's good. My next doctor's appointment is in another two weeks, but everything seems to be going fine."

"Good, good." Jagger bobs his head. "If you need anything, money or anything, just let me know."

I twist in my seat to study him. His usual light-hearted expression is serious. "Why?" I know the question is blunt, but after a lifetime of watching my mom being let down by men, it's hard to wrap my head around the fact that good guys exist.

"Sierra," he scoffs. "You have to ask? We care about you."

I bite my lip, wanting to question him further. I wait until he turns onto the highway before saying lightly, "Good to know."

"You know, when you first said you were pregnant, there was a moment when I thought it could be mine," Jagger said. I bug my eyes at him, but he's focused on the road.

"Did I scare you?"

"No," he says quickly. "No. Well, a little. But the main feeling wasn't panic. It was excitement."

I nod slowly, turning his words over carefully, checking them for subtext.

"I mean it." He glances at me for such a long time, I want to snap at him to watch where he's going. "There's not a guy there who wasn't wondering what it'd be like to be the father."

"Maybe not Roy and Tommy," I mumble, and he laughs.

"Okay, maybe not them. I'd have to ask them. But seriously, Sierra, we're all glad you're with us."

"Even if my pussy's about to get all stretched out," I try to joke, but can't bring myself to smile.

Jagger rolls his eyes. "I get you don't want our charity. But has it occurred to you that our lives are better because you're in them? Not just your fantastic pussy. You."

I cock my head to the side. "My pussy *is* fantastic."

"All right." He shakes his head as if to say, *Go ahead, keep joking. I'm trying be sincere.*

I let a mile pass before I say quietly, "I know what you're saying, and I appreciate it. It is hard for me to accept charity. And... I like keeping things simple. A child changes everything."

"Change isn't necessarily bad."

"No." I ponder this. What will be changing? Lincoln will still be protective, Saint subtly dominant. The twins and Jagger still try to draw me out and make me laugh and have fun. Even Mason still pretends to scowl at me. I haven't had sex with them since the announcement, but that was my choice. I could return to their beds in any moment and they'd welcome me. Or not, and they'll just cuddle and spoil me.

So far, all the changes have been good.

"I know you might not stay with us," Jagger says. "But it's great having you around. Not as a ready lay. As... as a woman. A friend."

I clear my throat. Damn hormones, making me teary every other minute. "Thanks, J. That means a lot."

He shrugs. Leaning over, I peck him on the check, eliciting a familiar giggle.

"Besides"—I settle back into my seat—"second trimester hormones are supposed to be insane."

He smirks. "Something to look forward too."

After filling the backseat with shopping bags, Jagger checks his phone. I wait while he texts someone. The air is crisper than I remember. It's been so long since I've ventured outside; I need to get out and get some exercise. I can do regular walks through the forest if the guys will show me a trail.

"Hey, you hungry?" Jagger asks, his eyes still on his phone. "We can stop for food before we head back."

I shrug. "I could eat. But Saint is cooking tonight, and I want to have an appetite."

"All right. One more errand, and we'll stop for gas and snacks before heading back."

When we're back on the road, a motorcycle rumbles by and I shrink down in my seat automatically. My memory of Jack's death seems so far away.

"I gotta be careful of these potholes. Hit one the wrong way and you might give birth."

The car stops and I sit up straighter, recognizing the hotel where I fucked Lincoln.

"It's okay, Sierra. Just a quick stop." Jagger winks at me, and lopes off. Saint hinted about Jagger's drug use. I wonder if the blond has a hookup in town. The last time I used anything was with the Hell Riders.

I slump in the passenger seat and let my eyes drift close. Memory whispers in my ear, my voice, strained and slurred. *"What did Dex want?"*

Jack fiddles with his beer bottle a moment before setting it aside. "Nothing, baby. Just club stuff." He tugs my hand and pulls me into his lap. I perch stiffly on his knee, refusing to relax as he massages my breast.

"You sure?" I glance at the door. I made sure Dex was gone before coming inside, but it's his place. He could return at any moment. "He's the president of the club. He scares me."

"Nah, he's good. Come on, S'erra." He hiccups. "I've got some stuff for us to try. Dex says we can use his back room."

I let him lead me down the hall. The walls are old-fashioned wood panels, once nice, now stained. It's still a nicer place than anywhere else I've lived.

Jack pulls me into a dark room and onto a bed. It smells like stale cigarettes, but the blanket's soft and warm. I snuggle into my boyfriend and give myself to trust. In a minute he'll give me a taste of whatever the Riders are dealing, and we'll fuck each other through the high. I'll fall asleep against him until nausea grips me. I'll stagger to the bathroom, grab the sink and hang on, keeping quiet as heavy boots head down the stairs. They'll be a murmur of men's voices and then—

A gunshot jerks me awake. I sit up, blinking, mouth dry, heart slamming in my tight chest. It takes me a moment to realize it wasn't a gunshot, but the sound of a bike. The rumbles increase and I duck my head, nearly braining myself on the dash. The motorcycles roar past and I wait, counting to ten, then twenty, then a hundred. Jagger should be back by now.

What's happened?

I scramble out of the truck, which room did he go into?

"Jagger?" I call. "Where are you?"

"In here." I follow his voice to room sixty-one. The door is cracked. I push it open and freeze

"Hello, Sierra," Dex says.

9

S ierra

DEX IS a good-looking son of a gun, with a dark tangle of hair, knife sharp cheekbones and haunting blue eyes. The seams on his face and rough tan from a lifetime riding a bike under a sunny sky only add to the weight of his presence.

I'd call him hot, even handsome, if I didn't know what a mean snake of a human he was.

Call her inside, Jack. It's time to share. I remember his rasping voice, the smell of sweat and weed and raw hooch heavy in the air. And Jack stammering and dissembling, while I hid in the shadows wishing I was anywhere, with anyone, besides in the house that belonged to Dex and the Hell Riders. That's the trouble with saying no to the head of the club. His will was law.

Still is.

"Still pretty." He cocks his head. "Bustier than I last saw you. But still pretty little Sierra."

"We're here for the reward," Jagger voice comes, offbeat and off-key. I barely hear him with the rushing in my ears. Dex's icy gaze on mine.

"Oh, J, what have you done?" I whisper. I knew he was a dense pothead, but I didn't think he'd sell me out.

"It's cool," Jagger says with a grin. "Your uncle just wanted to make sure you're not really missing. Tell him you're fine and we can get the reward and —"

"Jagger." I fight to keep my voice steady. "This is a mistake. You need to leave." It's too late for me, but maybe I can save him.

"I thought you'd want to see your friends," Jagger tells me. I shake my head at him, sadly. Stupid, superficial Jagger, just like so many men my mother and I trusted.

My heart was breaking. This would be the last time I'd see anyone. Dex was gonna take me into the back, and do whatever he wanted with me. I might survive. I might not.

"It's not what you think it is. You gotta leave, Jagger. Please," I break down and beg. Dex liked women to beg. He might show mercy.

Jagger thrusts out his chin and faces Dex. "You got her stuff?"

"No, but I brought money," Dex says in a neutral tone I don't trust at all. He grabs a duffel from the bed and tosses it Jagger's way.

Jagger catches it. "See," he turns to me with a big, dumb smile. "This will help you—"

The gunshot catches him mid-sentence. Jagger stutters, eyes wide, and folds over slowly.

I scream and fall to my knees by his side. "Jagger? Jagger?" I repeat his name as I pat his face, brushing back dirty blond locks to see if he's still with me. Blood seeps onto the floor. I'm kneeling in it, trying to stem the tide. Breath rattles in Jagger's chest, red saliva bubbling from his lax mouth. I watch as the light slowly slips from his eyes, weeping with my eyes open. It's Jack dying in my arms all over again.

"Sierra," Dex says from far away.

I close my eyes, tears running down my face in earnest.

"Sierra. Get up."

"What does it matter?" I rasp, my bloodstained hands over my belly as if to protect my baby. "You're just gonna kill me anyway."

"Not necessarily." Dex sits with the gun propped on his knee, casual as if nothing happened. He can kill a man and order pizza in the same breath. Evil is ordinary for someone like him.

"Not the brightest bulb," Dex mutters, mocking the man he just shot. "Sierra, be a good girl and fetch me the bag." He motions me to come, not worried at all that someone might call the cops. He knows the Riders control this town, and put him above the law. Holding my breath, I grab the bag and bring it back. I'm his bitch now. Until he plans to let daylight into my torso like he did Jagger's, which he could at any time. My tears are not for me, not really. I knew it could end this way at any time.

I only wish I could save my child.

"You won't get away with this," I tell him. I'm dead anyhow, so...

"Get away with what?" Dex asks like there's not a man bleeding out on the floor. "This? I can and will. My dear, I've been looking for you everywhere."

I shake my head.

"But yes. We were worried, so worried, when Jack turned up dead."

"I don't know what happened," I say in a rush to defend myself. "I heard a shot, and he was dead."

"Shhhh, I know. I know."

"You told everyone I killed him." I bite the inside of my cheek to keep from screaming, *Did I? What happened?*

"You don't remember that night?"

I shake my head. "I remember being outside. Then coming in." *After you left,* I add silently. "We drank more and took... something. I woke up later and threw up in the bathroom. But then..."

Boots in the hall. A measured voice. A gunshot.

"You really don't remember." Dex half chuckles. "Well, now, isn't this an interesting turn of events."

"I found him dead," I say shakily. "I heard the shot, but I wasn't in the room. I don't know what happened. We were in your house, and Jack was loyal to the club."

"Was he? Or had he turned traitor?" Dex lifts a brow. "Guess we'll never know."

The truth hits me so hard I rock back on my heels. "You killed him."

"Well, why would I do that?"

"You wanted him to share me," I whisper, feeling the shame as I did that night long ago. Just looking at Dex, I want to take a shower and scrub my skin inside and out.

Dex jiggles the gun. "You didn't want the threesome. But you were his property, and all Rider property ultimately belongs to me."

"I don't," I whisper. "I didn't belong to him. I didn't belong to anyone."

"No? I hear you've done all sorts of entertaining at the

lumberjack camp." Dex motions to Jagger's limp form on the floor. "This one told me."

I close my eyes and shake my head. "What are you going to do with me?"

"That depends on how you behave. What do you think, Sierra? Can you be a good girl?"

I lick my lips. "It doesn't matter. The club thinks I killed Jack. You told them."

He shrugs. "Stories can change. I think we can come up with something different to tell them."

I shake my head again, slowly. "You needed him to die for some reason. And I was a convenient one to blame." I bit my lip as I watched him toy with his gun. What could I say to get him to spare my life? How do you reason with a psychopath?

I locked my knees, forcing myself to stay strong. "Why did you kill him, Dex?"

The club president's eyes glitter. "He was selling out. Going to the cops, dealing to club enemies. He was trying to get out of the Riders." His brow creases as he studies me. "Maybe it was for you."

The words hit me and I stagger a little. Jack and I had talked about a different life, about running away and starting over. I didn't realize he meant it.

"Yes," Dex murmurs. "He didn't tell you, but he was turning over a new leaf. Once in a while, one of my men gets enamored with pussy, makes all sorts of promises. It always ends the same. I catch wind of it and"—his smile is horrifying—"drag him back to hell."

"Murderer," I mouth the words. I have no courage left shout accusations, or even say them. *Jack. Oh, Jack.*

"Enough now," Dex commands. "Time to come here, and convince me to spare your life."

I hesitate, knowing there's nothing I can say or do to convince this evil man that I should live. Any begging is an exercise in futility. But each remaining moment is precious. If I can delay my death even an hour, I have to try.

Before I can take a step, the door flies open behind me and a shot rings out. Dex jerks, his own arm spasming with the gun. A shriek escapes me as a hard arm wraps around my middle and yanks me back.

Mason's face fills my vision.

"Come on," he barks, and pulls me outside. He's pushing me, we're running down the long outdoor walk past hotel doors, shut tight, deaf dumb and blind to the violence going on inside.

"Come on." Mason drags me the final few feet when I would fall to the ground, wheezing for breath. "Get in the truck." I scramble in the driver's side, and settle. Mason has the ignition on and hits the gas before his door is even closed. I hang on, gritting my teeth and panting, every molecule in me fighting to hold it together as Mason guns the truck through town.

In the distance, bike engines roar. A storm of motorcycles, blowing through town. Any minute they'll realize their prez is dead, and start combing the country for the object of their revenge.

"You killed him," I hear myself say.

Mason doesn't answer. His jaw clenches as he takes a hairpin turn. The truck flies around and squeals forward. At one point, I swear we're on two wheels. My fingers will leave permanent marks where I'm gripping the handle.

By the time we hit the town limits, it's full dark.

"Mason," I gulp. "Jagger—"

"I know," he says. "I saw him."

I study his profile in the gloom, the sharp line of his jaw

silhouetted in shadow. He looks as fierce as he ever did. Does he still hate me? It's my fault his friend is dead. He probably hates me again, if he ever stopped.

The miles fly by, marked by black forest. *Where are you taking me?* I want to ask, but I don't know if he'll answer, and I don't want to make him mad.

I swallow and ask in a small voice, "How did you know how to find us?"

"Followed you from the store. I drove to town after I heard he took you. Jagger suddenly had a phone and reception; I knew he was up to something. He used to deal, figured he was at it again."

"Dex killed him. Jagger asked for the reward. Dex gave it to him, and then shot him." I shut my mouth tight. There's no reason for Mason to believe me. In fact, he should blame me for Jagger's death. I blame myself.

I fall silent as Mason drives like a demon down the long, dark road. The pines press closer and closer to the narrow strip of pavement. I've never seen such a dark night, the shadows pressing in until I can't breathe. Not even the night Jack died. That night is sealed in the sepia of my memory, lit by the yellowed street light and the dull glow of cigarettes smoked by the bikers who waited outside the house, calling for my blood.

Tonight is big and empty as the wilderness and the mystery of where Mason is taking me. I have no idea where we're going. My body cramps from bracing. I'm crammed into the corner of the seat, staring blindly into the dark as the truck hurtles closer to the middle of nowhere. Questions claw my throat; I swallow them down. I vacillate between shock, terror, and relief, but as the miles stretch on, fear crawls up from my heart, burning my throat like acid. Mason still hasn't said anything about where we're going.

But we can't drive forever. On the dash, the gas gauge needle wavers, dipping toward empty.

It occurs to me that Mason might have found a way to take care of all his problems. He's got a truck, and a dead man's posse on his tail. I'm the only witness to everything. He could easily get rid of all the evidence. He's got a gun, but he doesn't even have to kill me. Just has to drive me into the wilderness and leave me to die.

My mouth is too dry for me to cry out when Mason slows the truck, pulling onto the rocky shoulder and braking to an abrupt halt. I'm a statue in the seat as he exits the car, and comes around to open my door. "Get out."

Numb, I peel my fingers off the oh-shit handle and edge of the seat. He has to help me down, and still I stagger, legs cramping.

"Come on," he orders, and marches me into the forest.

This is it, this is it. I tell myself to run, but I can't. We're deep in the forest now, our boots kicking up wet leaves. Mason guides me by some invisible compass, weaving through the brush and wilderness as branches tear our legs and arms. We walk up a hill and down into a ravine, following a stream. I blunder along best I can, wondering if I'll have a chance to get free. Mason keeps his grip on me.

At last, we climb a hill. I jerk when I realize there's a tiny building up ahead.

"Not far now," Mason murmurs. Bile gnaws my insides again. My breath escapes me in a ragged rush.

My feet turn to concrete as we approach the small, dark shack. It looks like the perfect place for a serial killer to live. Home sweet home.

Mason has to drag me forward the final few feet.

"No," I fight and claw at him. It's no use. He's too strong. He hauls me through the door and fumbles on the wall for something. A second later, a flame flares, illuminating the harsh planes of his face. He holds a lantern. Doubled over, I catch my breath as he uses his lighter to get the kerosene soaked wick to catch. He hangs the old-fashioned light overhead and steps around it to loom over me. The small light makes his shadow double. Fuck, he's between me and the door.

I launch myself at him with a hoarse cry and he grabs my arms, stopping me easily. He stares down at me with such malice I flinch as if he's about to strike me down.

"Sierra, what the fuck?"

"Are you going to kill me?" My voice is strangled.

Disbelief wars with anger. "Is that what you think this is? I saved you from that biker fuck to drive you out here and kill you?"

I don't answer, trying to tug my wrist free. He pulls me forward, shackling both wrists and glowering at me until I stop fighting.

"I'm not the monster you think I am."

"Could've fooled me," I snap back. I must be out of my mind.

Mason just stares at me, dark eyes fathomless, mouth rigid.

"Just do it," I hiss.

"Sierra." He shakes his head, his thick dark hair waving. "I'm not gonna kill you."

Despite myself, I slump, like a puppet whose strings have been cut. "No?"

"No. That's not why I barged in and shot a man. I did it to save you. To get you out."

I'm crying again. My bones are liquid with relief. I lean against Mason's strong form as my own body turns into a fountain of tears. "You... you don't hate me?" I ask between blubbering.

"No," he answers cautiously. His fingers touch my face, hesitant as they brush away a few tears. "Is... is this hormones?"

"I don't know." I cry harder.

"Shit," he says and folds me in his arms. He's not as big as Lincoln or Saint or the twins, but there's plenty of strength in his lean body. "I don't want anything to happen to you. I don't want you to die."

I swallow my sniffles, forcing myself to get under control. Mason's shirt has a wet patch where I hid my face. "The club will come for you. Dex was the president. They can't let an outsider get away with killing him, even if it was self-defense."

Mason's face is in shadow. "I know."

"Well"—I wipe my eyes—"what now?"

10

S ierra

MY BREATH IS RAGGED as I follow Mason up the hill. He helps me over a fallen, moss-covered log, and lifts me when my boots would sink into a muddy patch near a grove of ferns. It's a long hike from the cabin to where we are, and it feels like it's all uphill. My muscles are screaming.

I have to remind myself that this was my plan all along—to spend more time getting exercise outdoors.

"You all right?" Mason asks as I pause, sucking harsh air into my lungs. Gulping, I nod.

He takes my hand and guides me around a downed tree. "We're almost there."

The first sign of our destination is a glimpse of yellow-orange between the trees. As we tromp forward, large pieces of equipment come into view, sitting at the end of freshly scored tracks in the black mud. The first guy we see is Oren, his red hair waving like a flag as he climbs the rise to where we stand.

"Hey," he greets us, and pulls me into a hug. I'm cold, my limbs are chilled from sleeping in the shack huddled in Mason's arms. We both woke before dawn and started hiking here.

Lincoln and Saint arrive next. The big black guy hands Mason a bag. "Change of clothes, food, more kerosene," he says.

Mason nods and checks it.

"How did you know?" I ask, teeth chattering from adrenaline. Lincoln pulls off his jacket and wraps it around me.

"Heard some talk on the police scanner. Shooting in a hotel. Two men gunned down. One gun found on scene. The other... no trace. The murderer ran. Pinning it on a club—the Hell Riders. Witnesses said they saw a guy looking like Mason and a girl looking like you at the scene."

"It was us," Mason says. "Club prez shot Jagger, was gonna do the same to Sierra. I interrupted. Shot him and got out."

"Yeah, I figured." Saint treats us to one of his impenetrable stares. "Time to gear up. You better go back into hiding. You got everything there you need for a few days." He points to the duffel bag he brought.

'You gonna run?" Lincoln asks.

"There's no time," Saint replies before Mason can answer. "They better hide."

"What about you guys?" I ask.

Mason and Lincoln exchange glances, communicating silently.

It's Saint who answers, crossing his arms over his chest. "The Riders want a fight, they'll get it. We prepare for war."

I bite my lip. "You should go. Tell them I ran. Don't you understand? You're in danger."

"Shhh, girl," Saint rumbles.

"It's okay, Sierra," Lincoln starts.

"It's not okay! They'll come after you—all of them. They won't stop until they take me."

"They won't take you. Not without a fight." Lincoln steps into my space, tips my chin up to look at him. "We're gonna protect you. I told you from the start."

I shake my head. "I don't want you to do that. I don't want you guys to get hurt." I glance at Oren, pleading. "Please don't do this."

"We have to," Lincoln starts.

"You don't. You can let me go."

Mason growls at that. I drop my eyes to the leaves at my feet.

"That's not an option," Lincoln tells me gently. "Even if you have to run, we'll follow. We'll stay with you."

"But why?" I blurt.

Lincoln turns me to face the rest of the guys, supporting me with one hand while the other slips over my belly. "We stick together. That's what families do."

My mouth falls open. Oren grins at me, and Saint's lips curl up slightly. Even Mason is nodding.

"He's right, Sierra." Mason steps forward to fix my collar. When he's done, he strokes his finger over the apple of my cheek, adding, "You're one of us."

AFTER THAT, the guys kiss me, tucking my hair carefully under my hood, and send me off with Mason's arm around my shoulders. We're to hike back to the cabin, settle in, and wait.

In the end, we don't have to wait long. A week after Dex and Jagger die, Elon and Oren roar up on ATVs. I ride back with my heart in my throat. As soon as we turn into the yard and I see the guys standing next to a big bonfire and a stack of motorcycles, I'm on the edge of my seat. Elon brakes and I practically leap into Lincoln's arms.

"It's all right." Lincoln's eyes are shadowed, tired. His clothes are dirty, and his beard is ragged with neglect. But he's alive. And so are the rest of the guys.

I ignore the tangle of axes beside the fire. If I'd looked closely, I'd see the sharp edges stained with blood.

Later, they tell me how it all went down. How Saint planned the whole operation and Lincoln oversaw it. How they dragged logs into the roads and laid long branches as traps and barriers over the largest potholes. While Mason and I waited, hunkered down in the cabin together, the motorcycles had come roaring up the road, only to be stopped by the debris. Some of the Riders had trucks that rolled forward, only to be stopped by the biggest logs.

They didn't tell me the rest—but I guessed. How they waited for the Riders to stall out, then fired warning shots from the yard. When the Riders drew their guns and started shooting, the lumberjacks returned fire. Shots flew into the trees on either side of the road and struck the logging equipment. None of the bikers got very close to the guys hiding in the woods. One guy almost reached the gates of the yard, but he'd run out of bullets. And one of the lumberjacks was waiting with an axe.

Whoever lived, fled on foot, leaving bodies behind. Elon was clipped by a bullet, but there were no casualties on the lumberjacks' side

After that, there was only clean up. The guys dismantled the bikes and towed away the trucks to prise apart and hide. Some parts they salvaged. Others they destroyed—made quick work of it with their machines and axes.

They buried all the bodies deep in the woods.

I hold Lincoln's hand as he tells me the story. My other hand covers my belly as if to protect my child from such a dark tale. It's something out of Brothers Grimm. At the end, when he falls silent, I kiss him.

"You're safe," he says. I caress his jaw, sifting my fingers through his silky black beard.

"Thanks to you."

His head drops for a moment, his brow pressing against mine. "You can stay now."

"Yes." I swallow, digesting the heavy truth. These men killed for me. We're bound together, now.

"You'll stay," Lincoln says. It's not quite a question.

I nod.

It might be best for us to go away. Find another company, and another camp. But we'll stick together. Home is where they are.

I belong with them. And they belong to me.

That night, after dinner, I turn on one of Jagger's playlists and dance. *Lovestoned/I Think She Knows* by Justin Timberlake. *See You Again* by Wiz Khalifa and Charlie Puth. *Put Your Lights On* by Santana and Everlast. The men watch quietly as I twist and turn and drop my clothes. And if I cry a little, it's for the ones who are not here. Tonight I dance in their memory.

The last note dies. Before the men can stir, I head to Lincoln. He scoots back from the table to welcome me and I lean into him, smelling the wild scent of earth and sky. I brush back his thick hair from his brow, bend and give him a soft kiss. My fingers go to the button on his jeans. He makes a small noise, but sits back, letting me open his pants. My arms go around his neck as I straddle him.

Are you sure? Lincoln's eyes ask.

Yes, I drag my hips up and down, rubbing against him before tugging my panties to the side and sinking down on him. *I'm sure.* I've never been more sure of anything.

I fuck him slowly, gritting my teeth at the stretch, a low hum in my throat at the delicious feel of him filling me.

"It's been a while," he gasps.

"Yeah." I nuzzle his neck. We rock and shudder together. I squeeze my muscles around him, and his head drops, his lower half jerking as he fills me. "Thanks," I murmur, and give him a kiss.

"Anytime," he mumbles with a laugh.

Around the table, the guys have their cocks out.

"Table," I murmur and Lincoln rises, lifting me up, laying me down. I reach for Elon, who already fists his cock. I watch him jerk off, admiring his freckled forearms, sleek with muscle covered in hair the color of rust. It doesn't take me more than a grunt to convince him to let me suck him. As I do, Oren approaches the foot of the table and grasps my hips. The two dip in and out of me, filling my sight and senses until I'm shuddering between them. They cum with a cry, and retreat, leaving me shivering, ready for my own climax.

"My turn," Mason growls. He pulls me to the edge of the table, flips me around. Bent in half, I grip the wooden edge helplessly as he pounds me from behind. The guys surrounding us murmur nervously. *Faster, harder,* I pant soundlessly as bright lights flash behind my eyes. My orgasm hits, rolling up from my core to my head, curling my toes. I sag and Mason grips my hair, making my body bow backwards as he plows my pussy. I dance on the end of his cock, jolting as electric pleasure sings through my limbs. Mason wraps an iron arm around my waist, holding me upright as he finishes, groaning. As I slump in his arms, he tugs my head to the side and fastens his mouth to my neck, sucking and kissing and claiming.

I'm shaking when he lets me go. Saint is there, touching me with caring fingers, offering me a glass of water.

"You ready, girl?" he rumbles, and I nod. He helps me up onto the table, lays me down on my back with my head hanging off, cradled in his hands. Slowly, he presses between my lips. The guys around us murmur in awe as I swallow Saint's monster like I've been trained. "Fuck," someone mutters. Maybe Tommy, or Roy. They're in the corner together, stealing secret kisses while I share my body with the rest.

Saint glides in and out, plumbing deeper with each stroke. A touch between my legs makes me jump.

"Easy, girl," Saint soothes. Someone's leaning over me, strumming my clit, urging me to climax. Saint bows over me, palming my right breast, then my left,

Then I'm dreaming, suspended in time, as the twins come and clean me with soft washcloths. Saint strokes my hair, murmuring, "Good girl." Mason brings a blanket, and Lincoln lifts me in his arms, and carries me to his room where we'll sleep. I close my eyes and let it go, because I'm not worried about missing anything now. Tonight is not the end of my time with the lumberjacks.

It is the beginning.

EPILOGUE

S ierra

"I CAN'T BELIEVE you're a mother." The blond guy on the computer screen laughs and shakes his head.

"Yeah, I know," I say. "Our mom would be grandmother. Can you imagine that?"

"She'd hate hearing that," the second guy says, leaning in front of his brother so he can see me. "She always made us call her Lynny. She'd probably make her grandkids do the same."

I roll my eyes, chuckling with the two guys. The Skype connection stalls for a second and I switch to the chat bar.

Losing connection. Maybe I can visit next Christmas. You can meet your niece.

That'd be great. The message pops up in the chat box, even as the image of the two guys freezes. Just in case they can still see me, I wave before I sign off.

"So they're your brothers?" Oren asks. He's sitting on the end of the table, working on a new carving project. His foot is propped on his last project, a beautiful cradle made from one giant piece of wood. He moves his foot absently, making the cradle rock, even though there's not a baby in there.

"Half-brothers. They're down in New York state." I close all the applications and shut the computer down.

Elon looks up from his knitting. He's got a large ball of yarn in the softest pink. I don't know what he's working on now—there's nothing more my daughter needs. He's already knit a hat, blankie and tiny sweater. "You've never met them, right?"

"Nope." That'll change. I want my daughter to know her family. I rise and head toward Saint's room. The door is cracked, so I knock.

"Enter." His deep voice reaches every secret part of me. I open the door and stand with the computer cocked on my hips. The big man is perched on the edge of his bed, boots planted on the ground, pink blanket spilling over his shoulder. One giant hand hides my daughter's lower torso. The other rubs her back. Nothing better than a big, beautiful man holding a baby. My ovaries sigh at the sight.

"She awake yet?"

"Nope." Saint cranes his neck to check on her. I set the computer down and creep around to see her peaceful little face. As soon as I see her, everything in me relaxes. I can't believe something so perfect came out of me. *We did good, Jack.*

My daughter's lips pucker into a little heart when she sleeps.

"You can put her down," I offer. "She'll stay asleep. Or if she doesn't, I'll feed her."

"I'm good," Saint says, and nods to the computer. "Did you like your gift?"

"Yes, thank you. I don't know how you found them. You work in mysterious ways."

Saint chuckles. "That's not your only gift."

When I raise my brows, he jerks his head toward a nondescript box next to him on the bed.

"What's this?" I ask.

"Another birthday present. We'll use it tonight."

I search his midnight dark eyes, my insides tingling. I've found the best sex toys come in bland packages.

"Better go rest up," Saint says. "I'll hold this baby. You take a nap. Later, you'll need it."

With a shiver and smile, I tiptoe out. Lincoln should be in his room.

Today was my birthday, and the guys went all out. In addition to all the baby stuff, Elon made me a matching sweater. Oren gave me a wood carving of a lithe little fairy holding a tiny blanket-bundled baby. Lincoln gave me a down coat and trapper hat made of faux fur. Roy and Tommy added to my music collection, and Mason gave me a new speaker system. Saint ordered me books and chocolate, and got the Skype connection to my half-brothers.

The guys made a chocolate sheet cake with a ganache topping too slick to stick a candle in, so they stacked biscuits into a pyramid and stuck candles in that instead.

I already have plans to express my gratitude. But first, Saint's right. I need my rest.

When I get to Lincoln's room, he's sitting propped on the bed, stroking his beard as he studies a report. His shirt is open halfway. When I knock lightly on the door, he turns to me and opens his arms.

"Did you enjoy meeting your brothers?" he asks, as I snuggle against him.

"Yes. I promised to visit one day."

"Good plan."

"I have no idea what to tell them about us. All of us."

He shrugs. "You'll think of something. I'm more worried about what you're going to tell Riley when she gets old enough to ask why she has seven dads."

"I'll think of something," I say, and yawn. I've already got an idea what I'll tell my daughter, inspired by some of the books I've read. As Lincoln wraps his arms around me, his beard tickles my cheek. I burrow into his hold and close my eyes to dream of the story...

Once upon a time, there was a young woman who ran from a bad man into a forest. The way was long and hard, but she soon came to a camp of lumberjacks living in the deep, dark woods...

ACKNOWLEDGMENTS

A huge 'thank you' to Maggie Ryan, who agreed to edit this reverse harem despite what I put her through with my first reverse harem, *Pearl's Possession*. You can thank her for this book having a plot.

Big hugs to my author friends, especially Aubrey Cara, who thought of this Hard 'n Dirty 'men at work' theme. To Stasia Black and Renee Rose, who gave me regular pep talks and kept me going. To my mom and sister for babysitting frequently. My husband and son, who offer hugs and breaks and laughter—you make it all worth it.

To Nanette and all the Goddesses who cheer me on, and all the readers who buy my books and allow me to love my dream.

And my new bebe girl, who napped and played quietly while mommy watched lumberjack documentaries and typed furiously...

FREE BOOK

Get a secret Berserker book, Bred by the Berserkers (only to the awesomesauce fans on Lee's email list)
Click here to get started...

EXCERPT: SOLD TO THE BERSERKERS

A MÉNAGE SHIFTER ROMANCE

By Lee Savino

The day my stepfather sold me to the Berserkers, I woke at dawn with him leering over me. "Get up." He made to kick me and I scrambled out of my sleep stupor to my feet.

"I need your help with a delivery."

I nodded and glanced at my sleeping mother and siblings. I didn't trust my stepfather around my three younger sisters, but if I was gone with him all day, they'd be safe. I'd taken to carrying a dirk myself. I did not dare kill him; we needed him for food and shelter, but if he attacked me again, I would fight.

My mother's second husband hated me, ever since the last time he'd tried to take me and I had fought back. My mother was gone to market, and when he tried to grab me, something in me snapped. I would not let him touch me again. I fought, kicking and scratching, and finally grabbing an iron pot and scalding him with heated water.

He bellowed and looked as if he wanted to hurt me, but kept his distance. When my mother returned he pretended like nothing was wrong, but his eyes followed me with hatred and cunning.

Out loud he called me ugly and mocking the scar that marred my neck since a wild dog attacked me when I was young. I ignored this and kept my distance. I'd heard the taunts about my hideous face since the wounds had healed into scars, a mass of silver tissue at my neck.

That morning, I wrapped a scarf over my hair and scarred neck and followed my stepfather, carrying his wares down the old road. At first I thought we were headed to the great market, but when we reached the fork in the road and he went an unfamiliar way, I hesitated. Something wasn't right.

"This way, cur." He'd taken to calling me "dog". He'd taunted me, saying the only sounds I could make were grunts like a beast, so I might as well be one. He was right. The attack had taken my voice by damaging my throat.

If I followed him into the forest and he tried to kill me, I wouldn't even be able to cry out.

"There's a rich man who asked for his wares delivered to his door." He marched on without a backward glance and I followed.

I had lived all my life in the kingdom of Alba, but when my father died and my mother remarried, we moved to my stepfather's village in the highlands, at the foot of the great, forbidding mountains. There were stories of evil that lived in the dark crevices of the heights, but I'd never believed them.

I knew enough monsters living in plain sight.

The longer we walked, the lower the sun sank in the sky, the more I knew my stepfather was trying to trick me, that there was no rich man waiting for these wares.

When the path curved, and my stepfather stepped out

from behind a boulder to surprise me, I was half ready, but before I could reach for my dirk he struck me so hard I fell.

I woke tied to a tree.

The light was lower, heralding dusk. I struggled silently, frantic gasps escaping from my scarred throat. My stepfather stepped into view and I felt a second of relief at a familiar face, before remembering the evil this man had wrought on my body. Whatever he was planning, it would bode ill for me, and my younger sisters. If I didn't survive, they would eventually share the same fate as mine.

"You're awake," he said. "Just in time for the sale."

I strained but my bonds held fast. As my stepfather approached, I realized that the scarf that I wrapped around my neck to hide my scars had fallen, exposing them. Out of habit, I twitched my head to the side, tucking my bad side towards my shoulder.

My stepfather smirked.

"So ugly," he sneered. "I could never find a husband for you, but I found someone to take you. A group of warriors passing through who saw you, and want to slake their lust on your body. Who knows, if you please them, they may let you live. But I doubt you'll survive these men. They're foreigners, mercenaries, come to fight for the king. Berserkers. If you're lucky your death will be swift when they tear you apart."

I'd heard the tales of berserker warriors, fearsome warriors of old. Ageless, timeless, they'd sailed over the seas to the land, plundering, killing, taking slaves, they fought for our kings, and their own. Nothing could stand in their path when they went into a killing rage.

I fought to keep my fear off my face. Berserker's were a myth, so my stepfather had probably sold me to a band of passing soldiers who would take their pleasure from my flesh before leaving me for dead, or selling me on.

"I could've sold you long ago, if I stripped you bare and put a bag over you head to hide those scars."

His hands pawed at me, and I shied away from his disgusting breath. He slapped me, then tore at my braid, letting my hair spill over my face and shoulders.

Bound as I was, I still could glare at him. I could do nothing to stop the sale, but I hoped my fierce expression told him I'd fight to the death if he tried to force himself on me.

His hand started to wander down towards my breast when a shadow moved on the edge of the clearing. It caught my eye and I startled. My stepfather stepped back as the warriors poured from the trees.

My first thought was that they were not men, but beasts. They prowled forward, dark shapes almost one with the shadows. A few wore animal pelts and held back, lurking on the edge of the woods. Two came forward, wearing the garb of warriors, bristling with weapons. One had dark hair, and the other long, dirty blond with a beard to match.

Their eyes glowed with a terrifying light.

As they approached, the smell of raw meat and blood wafted over us, and my stomach twisted. I was glad my stepfather hadn't fed me all day, or I would've emptied my guts on the ground.

My stepfather's face and tone took on the wheedling expression I'd seen when he was selling in the market.

"Good evening, sirs," he cringed before the largest, the blond with hair streaming down his chest.

They were perfectly silent, but the blond approached, fixing me with strange golden eyes.

Their faces were fair enough, but their hulking forms

and the quick, light way they moved made me catch my breath. I had never seen such massive men. Beside them, my stepfather looked like an ugly dwarf.

"This is the one you wanted," my stepfather continued. "She's healthy and strong. She will be a good slave for you."

My body would've shaken with terror, if I were not bound so tightly.

A dark haired warrior stepped up beside the blond and the two exchanged a look.

"You asked for the one with scars." My stepfather took my hair and jerked my head back, exposing the horrible, silvery mass. I shut my eyes, tears squeezing out at the sudden pain and humiliation.

The next thing I knew, my stepfather's grip loosened. A grunt, and I opened my eyes to see the dark haired warrior standing at my side. My stepfather sprawled on the ground as if he'd been pushed.

The blond leader prodded a boot into my stepfather's side.

"Get up," the blond said, in a voice that was more a growl than a human sound. It curdled my blood. My stepfather scrambled to his feet.

The black haired man cut away the last of my bonds, and I sagged forward. I would've fallen but he caught me easily and set me on my feet, keeping his arms around me. I was not the smallest woman, but he was a giant. Muscles bulged in his arms and chest, but he held me carefully. I stared at him, taking in his raven dark hair and strange gold eyes.

He tucked me closer to his muscled body.

Meanwhile, my stepfather whined. "I just wanted to show you the scars—"

Again that frightening growl from the blond. "You don't touch what is ours."

"I don't want to touch her." My stepfather spat.

Despite myself, I cowered against the man who held me. A stranger I had never met, he was still a safer haven than my stepfather.

"I only wish to make sure you are satisfied, milords. Do you want to sample her?" my stepfather asked in an evil tone. He wanted to see me torn apart.

A growl rumbled under my ear and I lifted my head. Who were these men, these great warriors who had bought and paid for me? The arms around my body were strong and solid, inescapable, but the gold eyes looking down at me were kind. The warrior ran his thumb across the pad of my lips, and his fingers were gentle for such a large, violent looking warrior. Under the scent of blood, he smelled of snow and sharp cold, a clean scent.

He pressed his face against my head, breathing in a deep breath.

The blond was looking at us.

"It's her," the black haired man growled, his voice so guttural. "This is the one."

One of his hands came to cover the side of my face and throat, holding my face to his chest in a protective gesture.

I closed my eyes, relaxing in the solid warmth of the warrior's body.

A clink of gold, and the deed was done. I'd been sold.

~

SOLD TO THE BERSERKERS

When Brenna's father sells her to a band of passing warriors, her only thought is to survive. She doesn't expect to be claimed by the two fearsome warriors who lead the Berserker clan. Kept in captivity, she is coddled and cared for, treated more like a savior than a slave. Can captivity lead to love? And when she discovers the truth behind the myth of the fearsome warriors, can she accept her place as the Berserkers' true mate?

～

Sold to the Berserkers is a standalone, short, MFM ménage romance starring two huge, dominant warriors who make it all about the woman. Read now in the Berserker Saga (on sale now):

Sold to the Berserkers

ALSO BY LEE SAVINO

Free book at www.leesavino.com

Contemporary Romance

Her Marine Daddy (free on all ebook retailers)

The Berserker Saga and Berserker Brides (menage werewolves)

Draekons (Dragons in Exile) with Lili Zander (menage alien dragons)

Bad Boy Alphas with Renee Rose (werewolves)

Made in United States
North Haven, CT
31 August 2024

56763363R00104